SHADOWS
OVER
THANKSGIVING

Jennifer J. Morgan

Books by Jennifer J. Morgan

Libby Madsen Cozy Mysteries

Shadows in the Forest
Spa Shadows
Shadowed Treasures
Shadow Retreats
Spooky Shadows
Shadow's Christmas Wish
Festive Shadows
Shadows in Alaska
Shadows Over Thanksgiving
The Christmas Fairy - a holiday novella

SHADOWS OVER THANKSGIVING

Libby Madsen Cozy Mysteries, Book 9

Jennifer J. Morgan

Secret Staircase Books

Shadows Over Thanksgiving
Published by Secret Staircase Books, an imprint of
Columbine Publishing Group, LLC
PO Box 416, Angel Fire, NM 87710

Book layout and design by Secret Staircase Books
First trade paperback edition: November, 2024
First e-book edition: November, 2024

Publisher's Cataloging-in-Publication Data

Morgan, Jennifer J.
Shadows Over Thanksgiving / by Jennifer J. Morgan.
p. cm.
ISBN 978-1649141996 (paperback)
ISBN 978-1649142009 (e-book)

1. Libby Madsen (Fictitious character). 2. Thanksgiving
holiday—Fiction. 3. Arizona—Fiction. 4. Amateur sleuths—Fiction.
5. Women sleuths—Fiction. I. Title

Libby Madsen Cozy Mystery Series : Book 9.
Morgan, Jennifer J., Libby Madsen cozy mysteries.

BISAC : FICTION / Mystery & Detective.

813/.54

For my dear friend, Aileen Brigman.
You have been my champion for nearly thirty years now …
listening while I cried on your shoulder throughout the dating and
child-rearing years. There for me as one of my mentors right from
the beginning of my corporate world ventures. Behind me whenever
my next crazy idea came around, including the one where I said, "I
think I'm going to write a book."
Not once have you discouraged me. In fact, your enthusiasm has
always been infectious. Continuously, you lift me and encourage me
to seek whatever I can dream up. You are a true treasure in my life
and I look forward to many more years of friendship.

* * *

Acknowledgments

After reading through a manuscript at what feels like a trillion times, I'm always surprised at how much I missed and how great my editors are. Beta readers—you rock! Enormous gratitude goes out to: **Lee Ellison, Sandra Anderson, Marcia Koopmann, Paula Webb, Susan Gross, Isobel Tamney, Eve Osborne, Dawn Hasiotis**.

I'm also sending gratitude to my author friends who inspire me, and have given me a lift with their support since I began this endeavor. It takes a village and I have such gratitude to the community of authors who all help one another succeed. **Thank you, Mary Seifert, Susan Yawn Tanner, Susan Slater, Jeffrey Poole, Connie Shelton, and Rebecca Barrett**. I'm honored to be writing along with these fantastic writers. If you haven't picked up their series yet, I strongly recommend you check them out.

PROLOGUE

She looked left, then right, carefully pulling out into the light traffic. This was an unknown area on the outskirts of town, but it was around here somewhere, she thought. Glancing at her Audi's navigational screen, it looked like she had several more miles to go and then she'd turn right again. There was another moment's hesitation; the same she felt earlier when she had agreed to dinner at his house, a man she'd only been around on a few other occasions.

She squinted to see the street signs. Headlights cut through the darkness with stark contrast, causing her eyes to avert. Miles down the road, with cars no longer in sight, the road stretched out ahead, a ribbon of asphalt disappearing into the inky blackness. This area in the Northeast valley sure seemed rural, yet she'd passed several extensive shopping areas only miles back. Nearly missing her turn, she slammed the brakes, skidding to a stop.

Letting out her pent-up breath, she questioned herself again as she made the turn. "Why drive clear across the city for this man? Aren't there plenty of men to date closer to where I live?" she chastised herself out loud, while looking around at all the beautiful houses that lined the street. "Well, he must have money to live in this neighborhood." She spotted the house number at the side of the garage and pulled into the empty driveway, not seeing a front door. Everything was pitch black. Unease gripped her stomach.

Pulling her phone out, she texted: I'm here. A chill crept down her spine as she watched the ellipses pulsate.

Great! Come on in!

Relief washed away her doubts, and she grabbed her purse, shoved her phone inside it, twisting around to look into the back seat. She shook her head and gave a chuckle. No, she'll leave it here for now—too presumptuous to show up at his door with an overnight bag. Another nagging feeling slowed her down as she opened her car door. She shrugged it off, whispering to herself, "It must be this darkness making my imagination run away, right? Settle down. This will be a great evening."

She locked her car and proceeded down a walkway, which snaked around before revealing the front door encased in darkness. She hesitated again as her eyes adjusted to the lack of light. With a deep sigh, her worries faded, seeing his bright smile greeting her as he opened the front door. His imposing height was yet again startling, although he was graceful and had a natural elegance that set him apart. Dark hair, almost raven-like, framed a face carved from stone, sharp angles softened by a hint of a beard. His eyes, the color of stormy seas, held a depth that drew her in. There was a quiet intensity about him, a magnetic pull that suggested a hidden world of complexity and passion.

"Sorry, I don't have shoes on or I would have come out to the car. And now I realize I forgot to turn on the porch light also," he said warmly, while lovingly reaching out for her hand. "Find your way, okay?" His hand settled in on her lower back, promptly ushering her inside the dimly lit home.

Her answer went unheard over the pulsating heartbeat pounding in his ears. Beneath his affable exterior lurked a darkness, a cold, calculating intelligence. His eyes, so warm and inviting only seconds before, held a chilling depth now, a predatory focus that hinted at a mind capable of great cruelty. It was this duality, this ability to be both captivating and terrifying, that made him so effective. His penetrating gaze glanced one last time over the neighborhood. No one was around.

Her car in the driveway would be a problem. He'd deal with that soon enough.

CHAPTER ONE

Aren't family gatherings meant to be joyous occasions? That's the picture I'd always held in my overly optimistic brain, anyway. Prior to my father's passing, I fondly remember several summers where we traveled back to the Midwest to visit his cousins at family reunions. As kids, my sister and I would run off with the rest of the children, which I guess were our second cousins, and we made it our job to stay away from the adults as long as possible. We'd play all day long, creating make-believe scenarios about how we were pioneers living off the land, only coming home when absolutely necessary—you know, to eat and sleep. It was so much fun; I have always cherished those memories. Maybe that's why I was so surprised by how much work went into planning and executing such a reunion as an adult. I certainly never considered this when agreeing to host Greg's family for Thanksgiving.

By the time we arrived home from our long drive back from Alaska several weeks prior, we had decided to host Thanksgiving at our home. I created lists: whom to invite and what food to serve. Looking back, that was probably the point where I needed to manage my expectations better. Now I only needed a glass of wine.

"Want something to drink? I'm pouring wine," I shouted to Greg, who had his feet up in a recliner in front of the TV.

"A beer would be nice. Thanks, sweetie!"

I poured a glass of Merlot and then grabbed him one of his lagers from the fridge and found the bottle opener.

"Here you go," I set it down on the small table to his left. During our recent trip, he'd broken his right arm. It took several weeks before they removed the cast. Now, he was finishing physical therapy and doing so much better. "Did you hear from Dana yet?"

"Not yet. Mom felt pretty sure she and the kids could come. They're probably still waiting on Joe's schedule to know whether he'll join."

I'd met all of Greg's family the previous winter when tragedy spoiled his college buddy's wedding in Taos, New Mexico. I looked forward to spending more quality time with them and getting to know his family better. Bill and Anne Lawson were your average seventy-plus parents who spent decades ranching in Colorado. His sister, Dana, worked in real estate. Her husband, Joe, was an airline pilot. Larry, Greg's younger brother, was an outdoorsman who had never quite settled down. During our first encounters, I found him to be very charming—quite the flirt. He was also a wanderer—never quite content where he was. Although he never settled on any one occupation, it seemed he made a fairly good living using his outdoors skills—skiing (snow and water), hiking, rafting, etc. He traveled many places and found work leading tours, and as an instructor in varying outdoor activities.

I sat down on the couch. "What are you watching?"

"Oh, I'm just flipping channels, really. Anything special you'd like to see?"

"There's a new season of *Bridgerton* on," I suggested.

He muttered something, rolling his eyes. "How about *True Detective* instead?"

"Sure, I love that series."

My black Labrador, Shadow, settled in at my feet. Greg found the channel, and we sat back, enjoying our evening drinks and watching TV together. Although I enjoyed the series, I found my thoughts drifting back to hosting guests and planning the enormous meal. At last count, there would be at least eighteen of us. My eyes scanned around the room, which was a combination of living, kitchen, and dining, all as one great room. Where would we fit them all?

My home was certainly modest sized, around fifteen hundred square feet. Plenty large enough for Greg and me. Still, it would be tight. My mind mulled that over and I never truly engaged in the detective show. Soon enough it was bedtime and thankfully, I slept well. I knew the days to come would be plenty busy.

The next day, after my morning's massage appointments wrapped up at the spa, Mom and I met over at my house.

"Maybe if you move the couch and recliners over here…" Julia walked to the far side of the living room, pointing as she went along.

"I guess for the meal, that'd be fine. But it won't be

convenient for football watching." I pointed out the wall-mounted TV.

"Ah, yes, I see what you mean."

We both walked through the room, turning this way and that, trying to figure it out.

"How many long folding tables do you have?" she asked.

"I've got two, besides our dining table. I *think* we'll be able to seat six at each folding table. So that will cover about twelve people. Then with the dining table, it could work. We might need to move a table outside, leaving the sliding glass door open."

"That would work. Maybe put the kids out there?"

"Yeah. It might be tight inside, but I think we can pull it off."

"Let's review the menu again. We'll divide and conquer on shopping."

"Oh, and don't forget the cooking sessions we'd planned at your house ahead of time. It'll be fun—a great time for us gals to spend time together."

Julia Madsen gave me one of her famous side-eyes. "A bunch of women in the kitchen? That sounds fun to you?"

I laughed. "It'll be fine. Lexi is always a great help. Jordan—well, at least she'll stay on task. I have no idea about Anne and Dana, but we'll see."

We sat at the kitchen table and reviewed the lists I'd compiled. Thank goodness for Mom. She noticed several things I'd missed and after revamping the shopping list, we had another entire page.

"When does Greg's family arrive?" she asked me.

"Sometime tonight."

Mom's eyes glanced across the room. "And they're

staying here?"

"No, heaven's no. They arranged for a vacation rental nearby. There's seven of them, Mom. We only have the two bedrooms."

"Oh good. That's one less hassle, anyway. Okay, we have exactly one week to get this meal together. Plenty of time."

After splitting the shopping list, Mom went about her day and I went back to work.

* * *

Cody, our new receptionist, greeted Shadow and me warmly as we walked in the door at Dharma Inspired Day Spa. Thankfully, the phone rang before he captured me in the lobby for too long. He had a way of pulling people into conversations, and it was difficult to get away. That wasn't a bad thing; his customer service skills were exemplary. However, I was already running late for my morning session with a client. Shadow stuck close by Cody, her newest buddy, because she was no dummy—he had a supply of dog treats in his desk drawer.

I hurried to my office, throwing my bag on my desk, before rushing out again. My business partner, Alexis Johnson, caught up to me in the hallway nearest the therapy rooms.

Lexi's aura was one of peace and confidence, a magnetic pull that drew people in. Dressed in flowing, earthy tones, she embodied that spiritual essence. Silver jewelry, adorned with intricate patterns, complemented her bohemian style. Her brilliant white smile and glowing cocoa complexion radiated her warmth.

"Hey, stranger. It's okay if Kathleen and Diane join us

next week, right?"

"Sure!" I agreed, quickly checking my watch. "Yikes, I'm late. Let's talk later, and I'll fill you in on all the plans."

"Okay, good. Hey, I'm taking off now. Call me when you're done," she shouted over her shoulder as she made her way to the lobby.

It felt as though the afternoon melted right into evening. At some point, I knew Greg had come by to pick up Shadow, but three massages later, I had completely lost track of time. By the time I finished cleaning massage tables and shuffling laundry, I made my way to the Serenity Room and poured myself a cup of tea. Silence filled the area and that's when I wondered whether everyone had gone home. I opened the swinging glass door and poked my head into the lobby. Beyond the front glass windows, darkness enveloped the parking lot, except for a few street lamps. The dimmed lobby lights showed me that Cody had already shut down his work area, so I closed the door and made my way to the back, toward the employee kitchen. A little flutter filled my stomach. The last time an employee was alone in the building, someone broke in and assaulted Lexi. From that point forward, we made a two-person closing rule.

Walking through the kitchen, I opened the door that led into the physical therapy unit next door. Healing Solutions was our tenant and a terrific health and wellness partner, as we frequently shared clients. Peering into pure darkness, I immediately shut the door and locked it, looking around our kitchen and seeing no one had cleaned up yet. I turned off the coffeepot and rinsed out the decanter, while trying to remember who was on the schedule to close with me tonight.

I strolled down the hallway leading to our offices,

calling out, "Anyone still here?" My words echoed off the walls. Silence filled in behind that echo. "Hello?" I tried again as I stepped into my office.

Quickly, I grabbed my purse, making sure my phone was still in there. I'd missed several calls. Greg, my mom, and my sister, Jordan. Sheesh. I pressed the button to play back the messages as I walked down the hallway, shutting off all the lights in the therapy rooms.

First my sister's message: "Libby, Apple is wondering if she can help you bake pies. I was sure that'd be okay. Just wanted to give you a heads up. What day are you planning on baking?" I smiled as I deleted. My twin nieces were two of my favorite people—Apple and Annie. I kid you not.

Next my mom's voice sounded: "Hey there, I have everything on my shopping list purchased now. Let me know what time to bring things over. That's tomorrow, right?"

Greg's message was more insistent. "Uh, hon. We have a huge problem. Call me the second you get this message." He'd left the message over an hour earlier.

A tremendous bang sounded from behind me. I jerked around, eyes wild, looking for the source. Cautiously, I stepped toward the kitchen. As I passed the opening for the Serenity Room, I caught movement.

"Who's there?" I shouted.

I caught a shadowed figure slinking through the darkness. I backed up a couple of steps and ducked behind the wall, even though I knew it was too late. My fingers fumbled with my phone, preparing to call the police.

"There you are, Libby."

"Cody! You scared the …" My heart pounded in my chest as I caught my breath.

"Sorry. I got locked inside Healing Solutions, but

thankfully I had the front door keys with me, to get back inside our part of the building. But we need to go lock their side of the building again."

I tossed my phone into my purse, then scolded, "Never scare me like that again. Didn't you hear me calling out?"

He shook his head and moved close, pulling me into a warm Cody hug. "I didn't hear you, love. Please forgive me."

He held me close with his typical warmth. Our receptionist was a man deeply in touch with his emotions; a heart he always wore openly on his sleeve. His eyes, a vibrant shade of green, often mirrored the depth of his feelings, reflecting joy, sorrow, or passion with equal intensity. His laughter was a contagious melody, and his smile, a sunbeam that could brighten even the gloomiest day. Everyone who knew Cody, or his husband, Brad, loved them immediately. It was impossible to stay mad at Cody for long.

I looked up at the six-foot-five tall young man and smiled. "Of course, I forgive you. Now, help me close up shop and let's get out of here."

A few minutes later, as I was rounding the corner to my house, my phone sounded through my hands-free technology in my car.

"Greg, I'm so sorry! Something…"

He didn't let me finish. "Libby. Where are you?"

"Just about to pull up at home. Is the family in town yet?"

"I'm going to drop you a map pin; follow it. I need you here quick—there's been a murder."

CHAPTER TWO

Averting my eyes from the flashing red and blue strobe lights, I carefully found a place to park several houses down from the address Greg had sent me. Greg's Tundra was across the street, as well as several police cars, both marked and unmarked. Fire department vehicles blocked the driveway and that's when I saw the coroner's van. With a glance to the left of the driveway, I saw JJ was already on scene as well, deep in conversation with another officer.

Detective Jeff Johnson, or JJ, as he's commonly known, had been my best friend since college. In fact, I still remembered that first time I introduced him and Alexis to one another. Of course, she was initially reluctant, but I saw it immediately. Their souls were entwined, like two branches of the same tree reaching for the same sunlight.

Physically, they couldn't be more different. His tall, sturdy structure with sensitive ivory skin and blonde cropped hair contrasted with her smooth, glowing ebony skin and dark curly hair. Alexis wasn't as tall as JJ, but at five-foot-eight, she wasn't considered short by any means. If he were part of the Hollywood set, he resembled Clint Eastwood's son. To me, she had the same essence as the gorgeous Zoe Saldana. But of course, the physical differences were superfluous. They shared an unspoken language, a silent communion of thoughts and feelings.

Knowing JJ as if he were my brother, I knew immediately something terrible had happened. The grim expression on his face made my stomach clench, wondering if the deceased was one of Greg's relatives. They'd checked into this vacation rental only hours before. *What on earth happened?*

I hurried from my 4Runner, jogging down the sidewalk, only to be thwarted by a young officer. I tried waving toward JJ to get his attention.

"Ma'am, this is a crime scene. I need you to get back in your vehicle."

"It's my family in there," I tried to explain, exaggerating the truth slightly. "Can I speak to Detective Johnson, please?"

"How are you related to the vic…"

Greg crossed through the home's desert landscape and quickly pulled me into his arms. Across the yard, I saw his parents talking to another officer. Relieved at seeing them, I kept my eyes peeled for the others.

"She's with us," Greg explained to the officer. "We won't go inside the house, but she needs to be with the family."

Hesitantly, the officer stepped aside and we crossed

through the same rocky terrain Greg had already navigated. His parents, Bill and Anne, reached out and embraced me.

"Oh, it was horrible, Libby!" she exclaimed.

Bill hung his head. "I don't know what we're supposed to do now."

Larry, Greg's brother, came up behind me. "Hey, good to see you again, sis!" He wrapped his arms around me from behind and lifted, squeezing a surprise squeal from me.

Once I had my feet back on the ground, I turned around to greet him. "Larry! Good to see you. But what's going on here?"

He shook his head, saying, "Someone had a really bad night." He chuckled, running his fingers through his long blonde hair.

Disgusted by his brother's nonchalance, Greg cut him off. "Larry, there's been a murder … some respect, please." His gaze went out to the street where all the neighbors watched intently.

Impatient with the lack of information I was getting, I turned to Greg. "Please—what is the story here? Who died? Where's your sister and her family?"

Bill cut in, "As we've told the police … we arrived a couple hours ago. Got the key from the lockbox there." He pointed to the front door. "The second we opened the front door, we knew something was horribly wrong."

"I thought someone left meat in the fridge and maybe the power had gone out," Anne explained, pinching her nose. "It was *rotten*."

Larry shrugged. "I knew it was a corpse."

Greg shot him another look, then turned to me. "Apparently, they found a woman in the bathtub."

"Dead." Larry punctuated the point for Greg.

"Yes. She was already deceased. In fact, they think she's been there for some time."

"Oh, my God." I couldn't believe what I was hearing. "I mean, doesn't a cleaning crew come in between tenants? How could she go undiscovered? I assume she was renting the place?"

Bill cleared his throat. "Those are all the same questions I asked. The police are trying to locate the owners of this vacation rental, so we know nothing yet."

"And where are Dana and the kids?" I still hadn't seen Greg's sister.

Bill pointed down the street. "A nice lady officer took them away from the scene. Thankfully, the kids are unaware of what we discovered. They're in that van down there until we figure out what to do next."

"Well, you all will come back to our house until we can figure out the next steps. Are you finished with the police?"

JJ walked up and I turned to him for answers. "Are they free to leave?"

"They will be soon. Of course, we're going to have them come to the station for formal interviews."

"Tonight?" Greg asked. "They traveled all day from Colorado."

"I'm sure we can arrange it for tomorrow. It's clear your family is not responsible since they only arrived this afternoon. I'm sure once we reach the property owners, we'll be able to validate the time of her arrival on those cameras." He pointed toward the house. JJ's phone chimed. "Listen folks, let me double check with the chief and then I'll let you know if it's okay to leave. They'll be staying at your address?" he asked me.

"Yes, of course." I sighed, not sure how to accommodate everyone comfortably in our home, but we'd figure something out.

I turned to walk back to my 4Runner just in time to see a gurney being loaded into the coroner's van.

* * *

Quickly dusting the guest room, I was thankful the linens were clean and the queen-sized bed had already been made. Anne and Bill would be comfortable for tonight, and then we'd figure out a longer-term plan. I had another queen-sized inflatable mattress that we set up in the living room, and we found enough sheets and blankets for the family to spread out on the sectional sofa as well. I'd learned that Dana's husband, Joe, wasn't due in until the following week, so for now she and her brother would share the sofa space. Dana's two children, Joey and Lila, were completely content on the inflatable mattress on the floor.

Dana walked up behind, startling me. "Got any wine, by chance?"

"Of course!" I turned and opened a cabinet and pulled out a couple bottles. "Red or white?"

She smiled. "That merlot looks great. Do you mind? It's been a day."

I looked around the room. The kids busied themselves with a movie on the TV; Lila was stroking Shadow's fur as they sat side by side. Greg had gone out to the garage for something, and I figured Larry followed him because I didn't see him anywhere. Anne and Bill had already called it a night and were in their room.

"What do you say? Let's pour us a glass and head

outside?" I asked as I poured.

"I would love some fresh air, and your Arizona weather is positively balmy for November. At least compared to ours in Colorado."

We each grabbed a light jacket and quietly snuck out the sliding glass door.

"I'm so sorry to put you out, Libby."

"What do you mean?"

"It's a lot to put up a household full of people at the last minute."

"Oh! No. Nothing you could have done about that. And I'm happy we've come up with something … I'm only sorry we don't have more guest rooms. We'll figure it out though, don't worry."

"I'm really not looking forward to more police interrogation. All this is freaking me out."

"I can only imagine. JJ is a good guy, though; don't worry."

"Yeah, I remember him from Taos … even though we spent little time around him and his wife, I really enjoyed the time we had. They'll join us for Thanksgiving dinner, right?"

"Oh yeah. You'll get to meet my family and all our friends. Hey, in fact, let me call the spa in the morning and see if we can get you in for a massage tomorrow. That should help you unwind from the stress."

"Ooooh, that would be fantastic, Libby."

"Do you think Anne would like that also?"

"I'm not sure that's her cup of tea." Dana shrugged. "Couldn't hurt to ask, though."

"Well, we'll see what we can work out. You all are here for two full weeks, so I'm sure whoever wants treatment can get it. What do the kids like to do? Maybe we can arrange some activities for them as well. My sister has kids around the same age."

"They'd love to mix it up with other kids. They're also easily entertained by video games and TV so please don't be concerned about keeping them busy."

As I thought through the lists I'd been making for the meal preparation; now that we had a houseful of guests, Greg would need to help me keep his family entertained and out of the house. I lifted the wineglass to my lips and took a nice, long sip. No sense getting worried yet; take things one step at a time, I told myself.

My phone rang.

"Hi JJ," I answered, and at the same time, looked over at Dana. "No, it's not too late. Greg's sister and I are sitting outside drinking wine."

He launched right in with the reason for his call—asking for Greg's family to be at the police station at eight the next morning.

"Isn't that awfully early?"

"I know. Sorry. But we need their statements—each of them—before the homeowners arrive around noon. Also, we were hoping to have the Lawsons here at the station for their arrival. Having learned the news, they are particularly concerned about their guests and wanted to speak to them in person."

"Sure, no worries. We'll get them over there." I said goodbye and ended the call. Turning to Dana, I sighed. "Well, we'll get the interview over with early tomorrow. Gotta be there by eight."

She looked at her watch. "Guess it's time for bed, then."

We finished our wine and walked back inside. The kids were fast asleep, and Larry was nowhere to be found. I whispered to Shadow, taking her outside for potty and then secured her in for the night, after giving the requisite cookie.

"Goodnight Dana. Tomorrow will be a better day," I whispered, before I walked down the hall to my bedroom.

CHAPTER THREE

Walking into the police station brought back memories. Only last spring, that arts and crafts festival was a crazy time. The scary part of that time was the fact that anyone would point fingers at me and say I poisoned dogs, or stole merchandise from fellow vendors—that was beyond insane. Thankfully, this time around, no one I knew was actually the law enforcement's target, so that was a relief. I kept myself calm by reminding myself that Greg's family would give their statements and we would leave. Simple as that.

Except that it wasn't that simple. Nothing ever is.

Greg and I waited for hours, seated in the hard plastic chairs in the lobby, while Larry, Dana, Bill, and Anne were called one-by-one to separate rooms for their interviews.

Dana's knee bounced up and down, nervously waiting her turn to be called.

Greg whispered to me, "That was really nice of Jordan to take my sister's kids for the morning."

"I think it helps to keep her own kids entertained, honestly. I only hope that everyone gets along and it goes well."

He nodded. "You don't think the kids know what's going on, do you?"

"Lila and Joey? Nah. Dana has really sheltered them from it all. I mean, they know *something* happened because the police showed up. But it sounds like Dana did well keeping the details from their little ears."

"I can't believe this happened. I mean, what are the odds someone checks into a vacation rental and finds a dead body?" He shuddered.

"I'd been trying not to think about it. Did JJ ever say whether she was the previous tenant?"

"I'm not sure they know yet."

There was a whoosh as the sliding doors opened nearby.

I stood up as soon as I saw who it was. "Melissa!"

She spun around. "Libby? What are you doing here?" Walking right over to me, she reached over and gave me a giant hug.

"It's a long story you'd never believe, but we're here with Greg's family." I stated matter-of-factly.

She scoffed, then retorted, "Not unless someone died in your bathtub! Now *that's* a long story I'm here to learn about." She realized quickly how horrible that sounded and her hand slapped over her mouth. "I shouldn't be so cavalier. It's absolutely horrible—but we need to find out exactly what happened."

Before I could ask more, her husband, Fred, reached out to shake my hand. "Libby, how the heck are you? How's that beautiful home working out for you? It's been a while."

"Doing well, Fred. Melissa and Fred, please meet Greg…" He stood, greeting them both.

Greg's face changed, looking solemn. "Did I hear you right, Melissa? A dead body in a bathtub?"

Her head hung before she looked him in the eyes. "Yes, unfortunately. Horrible. We're here to learn more from the police."

Greg cut in. "Yeah, family were your renters. This is, if you are the owners of the house on Lindley St.?"

"Yep. Oh, dear!" Her hand covered her mouth again. "Oh boy. We're terribly sorry for the inconvenience."

"Not like you could have prevented it, right?" I blurted out.

Both Melissa and Fred glanced at one another and then back at us.

"I mean, surely this isn't your fault, right?"

They chuckled uneasily, then Fred excused himself to tell the officer at the front desk that they had arrived. Melissa lowered her voice when answering my question. "They haven't told us much. Only that there was a deceased woman, estimated to be in her thirties, in the primary bathroom."

I nodded. "Had she rented the place from you?"

"I'm not sure they've identified her yet, but I don't think so. Our last renters were more of our age—in their sixties, anyway. Unless they had a younger friend or daughter who visited them? I don't think they had guests over, though. Anyway, that was around three weeks ago when they checked out. The cleaning company comes in the same day guests check out—and no one had informed us of any issues."

"Would anyone else come and go from the house between renters?"

"Well, of course, Tiago—he's our property manager. And like I said, they cleaned after the Smiths' visit. Nothing unusual reported then. Tiago had an outdoor water leak to fix—you know, those darned timed watering systems— well, he repaired that several days after they'd checked out. But, since then, no one has been in there. At least, so I thought." Sadness washed over her and she quieted.

"Had the police said whether it looked like someone broke in?"

Slowly she shook her head. "That's what was strange. They said there was a small back window broken, only it wasn't near a door where someone could get inside. And it was only a crack. Maybe that shows someone *tried* to break in? I don't know. Normally the alarm system would get activated with a break, but Fred checked with the company and there were no incidents."

I watched as Fred passed by us and took a seat next to Greg. I heard them talking softly when I asked her, "Do you live nearby?"

"Oh, we were at our home in Rocky Point."

"That's cool … I didn't know you had a place there."

"We're spending more time there than here these days." Wistfully, her eyes cast over to Fred. Then she quickly added, "It's a much better way of life."

"I was wondering why you hadn't been to see me in a while."

She reached for her lower back. "I know! I really

could use some work. The lady I have work on me down in Mexico is good, but I haven't found anyone who does Ashiatsu. This girl comes out to our house, though. It's convenient."

"Well, come by the spa while you're in town. We'll get you fixed up." I smiled. "It might have to be another therapist, though. I am in the midst of hosting Thanksgiving, and we have family in town for the next couple weeks."

"Oh boy. That's why Greg's family has come to town, isn't it?"

I nodded. "Yeah, we need to find them somewhere to stay, too. There are seven of them and last night we just sprawled them out wherever we found the room. In a few days, that won't work so well when we have to move furniture around just to fit the twenty plus people." As I said it, I remembered the few additions I'd agreed to yesterday.

"Oh wow. You're kidding me? Why would you do that to yourself? We're hoping to get this done, get a cleaning crew to the house, and then skedaddle back to the solitude in Mexico."

I laughed, inspired by her optimism. Then my phone rang. Before I could answer it, Melissa and Fred were shuffled away down the hall by a detective.

"Hi Mom," I answered.

"Libby, the kitchen caught on fire!"

"Call 911, not me!" I shouted, my heart pounding furiously. "Get out of the house!"

"Oh, we did, and it's out now. They are checking everything out, but it's a mess in there."

"Are you okay?"

"Oh, we're fine. But the oven—it's toast. And the walls

and counters are definitely smoke damaged, but I'm sure we can just wipe them down. No problem."

"We can replace ovens. We cannot replace you and Margie. What were you cooking, anyway?"

"We had put in a couple of pies. Wanted to get ahead on the baking."

"Mom! We don't need to start all that for several days."

"Well, you have your hands full with Greg's family. How's that going?"

"We're still at the police station. Once we're done, though, I'll come over and see what I can do to help you clean up. Maybe we'll head to the appliance store and see about getting you an oven."

"You don't worry about me now. Call me when you're finished there."

She didn't wait for a goodbye and just hung up. Greg stared at me, waiting for the explanation.

"Oh, well, she tried burning down her kitchen," I simply stated.

The chuckle escaped him immediately. "I only laugh because I gathered from the conversation that she is okay. What did she do?"

"I'm not sure, but now we need to get her a new oven. We're supposed to be using her nice double oven to prep most of the holiday meal ahead of time."

"Oh c'mon. It'll work out fine." He caressed my knuckles as we sat there, waiting for his family to finish their interviews. "How many people are coming, anyway? It can't be all that bad."

"Only a small army. Last count was twenty-three, I think."

He gulped, and his eyes bulged.

"Now who's laughing," I remarked. "I have no idea how we're fitting everyone, but we'll work something out." I looked up to see Bill and Anne coming toward us.

Greg rose, asking his father, "Everything okay? You don't look so well."

He cleared his throat. "Do you know where Larry went last night?"

I turned to Anne. Her watery eyes had widened, imploring her son for the answers.

Greg shrugged and mouthed to me, *do you know?*

I slowly shook my head. "Dana and I sat outside for a little while. Honestly, I thought he was with you. But, why? What's going on?"

Bill took a seat, lowering his head into his palms. When he looked up again, his eyes narrowed. "None of us saw him last night after we got back to Libby's and the police are asking questions. I'm not sure why, but I get the idea that he may have lied to them about his whereabouts."

I took Anne's arm when she appeared unsteady and helped her take a seat next to Bill. "So? What does that have to do with the body found in the rental, though? I'm really confused."

Anne was silent. Bill shook his head. "I don't like any of this. It's almost as though we're suspects now."

Greg pivoted to his father. "Did they say that, Dad?"

"No. But I'm not talking to them anymore without my lawyer present." He dug out his phone and began to scroll.

Anne squinted her eyes and meekly asked, "We have a lawyer?"

Never answering, he only focused on his phone screen. Greg and I cast glances at one another, not sure what to say. I was about to go ask to speak to JJ when he and Dana appeared from around the corner. She looked unfazed, and JJ was smiling. Certainly, the news couldn't be as dire as Bill and Anne projected.

"Hey, Libby!" JJ embraced me. "I didn't know you guys would wait around."

"How's the investigation going?"

"Oh, still early on, you know. Lots yet to learn." He looked over and saw Bill still grimacing and wringing his hands. "You doing okay, Bill?"

"Sure, sure." He shrugged and cast his eyes downward again.

I signaled to my friend to step down the hallway with me. "Are you in on these interviews?" I asked JJ.

"I interviewed Dana."

"Something disturbed Bill—they were asking where Larry was last night."

"Larry. That's Greg's brother, right?"

I nodded. "What does Larry's whereabouts have to do with the body at the rental?"

He shrugged. "Uh, I don't know, Libby. But I can ask the guys that interviewed Bill. I remember now that Dana mentioned something about not seeing Larry after you all got back to your house."

"I don't understand why the questioning revolves around what happened *after* we left the rental? Doesn't that seem strange?"

"Yeah, I guess so. Or Bill is overreacting. I mean, this is a highly stressful situation."

I nodded in agreement. "Oh! I didn't realize the Barnsteads own that property, but we saw them when they first arrived."

"You know them?"

I nodded. "So does Lexi. Melissa has been a client since we first opened."

He bit his lip. His brow furrowed, and I saw his jaw muscle tense.

"What is it?" There was definitely something he wasn't saying.

"How well do you know them?"

"She's been a client and, oh, he was my real estate agent when I bought my house."

"Not close friends, though?"

"No, not really. I hadn't known they're spending most of their time down in Mexico these days. Yeah it's been a while since I've seen her."

"Mexico, huh?"

"JJ! What is it? Are they suspects?"

"It's too soon to say. However, we're still sifting through evidence and I'll only say it's interesting they've been in Mexico."

Larry opened a door several down from where we stood. "Hey guys!" he greeted cheerfully. He and JJ shook hands and with the other, gave a slap to each other's back.

"Good to see you, Larry. Bet these two have a bunch of activities planned for your family while you're here. Sorry it's off to a rocky start."

I cringed, wondering if I would get roped into planning activities for everyone. Wasn't a huge family meal enough?

We strolled over to where everyone else was seated. Bill and Anne seemed to have lightened up, talking with their son. JJ excused himself when he got a text summoning him to the boss's office.

"It's nearly lunch time now. Shall we?" Greg asked.

"Why don't you take your family out for lunch and I'll

head to Mom's to see how bad it is over there."

He nodded and gave me a peck on the cheek before I walked out. I overheard him explaining about the fire to his mom as the sliding doors closed behind me.

Digging through my purse for my keys and walking through the parking lot, I slammed right into a dark, tall wall of pure muscle. My purse fell to the ground, several items slipped out. "Sorry! My bad. I should have been paying attention to where I was walking," I said, kneeling down to pick up my belongings, then looking up into the coldest eyes I've ever encountered.

He grunted some obscenity and stormed off.

My eyes followed him until he rounded the side of the police station, heading for the building next to it. Electricity stabbed from the center of my being, sending chills throughout my body. Unnerved, I took a moment to get balanced again and then quickly got to my car.

CHAPTER FOUR

Navigating through the streets out of downtown Mesa, my eyes darted between the road and the rearview mirror in a constant, frantic scan, absolutely certain someone was following me. Noticing my white knuckles gripping tightly to the steering wheel, I took in a deep breath and slowly released it. *What was it about that man that spooked me so?* The once familiar streets seemed like a labyrinth of potential threats. *I've got to calm down.*

Turning into my mother's neighborhood twenty minutes later, I had relaxed a little bit. One last glance in the mirror, I saw no one followed me onto her street. What was I so afraid of anyway? I mean, I watched the man walk toward the buildings. Presumably, he went inside one of them, so the chances that he could have returned to his vehicle, caught up to me, and followed me across town were very slim. Even so, in recent years, I've learned to pay attention to my intuition and heed its warnings.

Mom stepped out onto her front patio, waving at me. She wore the cutest pink polyester pants with a floral button-down shirt. Her mostly gray hair still showed glimpses of brown and today she had pinned the shoulder length hair back at her temples.

"What's wrong?" she asked the second I stepped out of my car.

Taking one last deep lungful of air and letting it out, I simply stated, "Traffic. No worries. How's the kitchen?"

She rolled her eyes as they began to tear up. "Well, we're not cooking here anytime soon. It's a mess—I can't believe this happened."

As I approached the front door, I could already detect the smoky smell. I noticed all windows and doors were wide open. I stepped inside.

"Hey, where's Shadow?" she asked.

"I've come directly from the police station, so she had to stay home. Plus, if we're going shopping for an oven…" My mouth stopped the moment my feet did. My eyes scanned the walls ahead of me, just past the living room. "What the … the fire came out past the kitchen?"

"Mostly smoke damage. And, just a little bit … well, most of it is in there," Mom added, directing me into the kitchen.

As I rounded the corner, my hand flew to my mouth. The damage was beyond comprehension. Black melted Formica countertops, a busted-out window above the kitchen sink, charred remains of who knows what, and charcoaled walls and cabinetry. "Mom…" That was all I could get out.

"At least the damage is mostly contained to the kitchen, and I'm thankful for that."

"How are you able to stay so calm?" The smell was abhorrent. There was no way she could stay in the house until the kitchen got fixed. My spirit deflated as I took in the magnitude. Buying a new oven was the least of the problem.

"C'mon, Mom. Let's get fresh air—you can't be breathing this stuff." As we carefully stepped through into her backyard, I noticed that the back door was dangling from its hinges. The pool deck chairs were strewn everywhere. Debris littered the pool. "Wow. You'd think there was an explosion."

"The firefighters were everywhere, but at least they saved the house."

My phone rang and I saw it was Greg. I held up my finger, stopping my mom while I answered it, and walked around to the side yard.

"How's oven shopping going?" he asked cheerfully.

"Uh, well … it's a little worse than that."

"Oh no, what do you mean? Is Julia okay?"

I assured him she was doing better than I'd be doing in the same situation and then explained what I'd seen inside.

"Well then, I may have good news for you. I think we've come up with a solution for housing the guests. I'm taking the family out to see our land. If they like what they see, I think it'd work out for them to stay in the trailer."

"Is that enough room for them?"

"We'll see. But, between that, and possibly another rental for Mom and Dad, then your mom could use our guestroom."

I liked the sound of how he was embracing '*our*' these

days, and surprisingly, for the first time, it wasn't freaking me out.

I simply replied, "Let me know how it goes. Then can you come by here? At minimum, we have to get a window and door sealed shut from the elements, so I could use a little muscle for that. In the meantime, I need to help Mom get insurance involved and a restoration company out here, too."

"Absolutely. I'll call when we're on our way."

We hung up and my brain filled with checklist items I needed to write down. I found mom back inside the house, this time on the sofa in her living room, bent forward with her forehead in her hands. I sat down next to her.

"I'm so sorry, Mom."

She sniffled. The weight of all that had happened finally hit her and she sobbed. "I'm so stupid. If only I'd waited for help instead of trying to tackle it all on my own. I mean, I only stepped out for a second. And I had no idea I'd stored a pan with dish towels inside that oven!"

My heart sank.

"Look, Mom. We're going to get this figured out."

"What about Thanksgiving?"

"Well, it is approaching. That's true. Let's take one step at a time, though. Where can I find the home insurance information? We need to call them."

She got up and headed down the hallway. After a couple minutes, she came back with paperwork in her hands.

"Okay, good. Now, let's go to my house and do this. Breathing in these carcinogens is not smart. Where's your purse?"

Mom cast her eyes toward the kitchen.

"Oh, dear. Okay. We'll use my keys to lock the front

door. Do you need a light jacket or anything?"

She grabbed one from a chair near the front door, and I led her out to my car.

Using my hands-free technology, I enunciated loudly, asking it to dial Greg. Before I realized, Cody from the spa answered the phone, "It's a beautiful day at Dharma Inspired. How can we make you smile?"

"Sorry, Cody. I was trying to call someone else."

"Libby!" he cheered. "I'm so happy you called. Where are you? Are you able to stop by?"

"Uh, not really. Why? Wait, what's that awful noise?"

"Yeah, that's the alarm system. We can't get it turned off. The police are here."

"Where's Lexi?"

"She's at Joshua's school this afternoon."

"I'm on my way..."

My mom shrugged her shoulders, rolling right along with the latest plan. I floored it and we made record time.

As I watched the last officer walk out the front door, I gave thanks for a couple of things. One, it happened during the slower hours. Most employees were on lunch break and no clients were in the building. Two, it was only a battery issue with the security system, meaning no one broke in through the back door, and it wasn't a fire alarm. Now that my heart rate came back down to normal, I decided we could use the office phones to make the insurance calls.

After being on hold for nearly twenty minutes, the intercom buzzed.

"Yes, Cody..."

"Libby, you have a client up front." Then, he cleared

his throat and I could picture him turning away from the client as he whispered, "I see nothing on the schedule for you today."

"Who is it?"

"Melissa Barnstead."

I handed the phone to my mother and walked up to the front desk.

"Melissa?"

"Hi Libby! You said stop by ... and oh, with all this murder business…"

I saw Cody's eyes widen as he failed in pretending to give us privacy.

"Let's step into the Serenity Room, Melissa…" I guided her in and offered a cup of tea.

"I can't believe they're going to make us stay in the U.S. until the investigation is over!" Melissa took a sip of tea and then continued to vent for the next fifteen minutes. "If Fred had only fired that guy months ago…"

"They think the property manager has something to do with the woman's murder?"

"Oh, no. Well, I'm not sure. But he never follows up, and it takes us several times asking for repair jobs to be done before he actually completes anything. I've not been happy with Tiago for a while now."

"Do you have any theories on what happened? Have you learned whether the deceased was related to your last tenant?"

Melissa whipped her head around, the chunky gold dangling earrings slapping the side of her face when she stopped. "They have identified her." She leaned in, whispering the rest, even though we were the only ones around. "I don't think they've notified next of kin, so don't say anything, but her name is Carol Linton. She was a thirty-eight-year-old mother of two."

"Oh, my…"

"Yeah, and the tragedy of it all is that they suspected *drugs*."

I shifted in my seat, thinking that the death was tragedy enough, no matter how it happened. "So are you saying they are backing away from murder and it could be an accidental overdose or something?"

"That I don't know. The way we got interrogated, it seemed to me they feel certain foul play was involved." She stood up and began pacing. "It's just too much. I can't handle all this—and at a time where I finally got my husband back and we're enjoying retirement."

My mom popped her head in the room. "Libby, they're asking questions I'm not sure about. Can you help?"

I told her I'd be there in a second. "Listen, Melissa, I can't help you today with a massage. You may make an appointment with Cody up front and maybe we'll have another therapist available for you tomorrow."

"Oh, Libby, I couldn't possibly see anyone but *you*…"

"Today, that's not possible. My mom's house caught on fire and we're dealing with that now. And along with family in town, planning a large holiday meal, I'm not available this week or next." I turned away when I saw her mouth turning down into a pout. "Here, let's see what Cody can do … I've got to get on the phone with the insurance company now." I walked her into the lobby and gave Cody instructions to arrange for the earliest possible massage.

"Take care, Melissa." I turned and hurried into the office at the rear of the building.

* * *

Seeing Greg's smiling face at home an hour later lifted my soul. He planted a big kiss on my lips, then launched right in with the updates.

"I got Larry, Dana, and her family all settled in the trailer. They're completely content. Mom and Dad are staying at a Best Western between here and there. For now, they're resting. I told them we'd contact them with a dinner plan before six."

A man who took care of things. I couldn't love him more, I thought, as I watched him take my mom by the elbow and guide her into the guestroom. Not that she was elderly or weak, but the day had exhausted her. I took my pup outside to do her business while Mom got settled in.

Greg set fresh towels on the dresser. "I washed everything and cleared the dresser drawers. Spread out and make yourself at home, Julia."

"I sure hope you are still planning the big surprise?" she winked.

"Shhh…" he nervously hissed, looking around. "Don't blow the surprise, please."

"Don't you worry. I've kept it secret all summer long, haven't I?"

"Barely," he quipped, remembering all the near misses. "Thankfully, she's been so distracted since we got back from Alaska. I accidentally left the little black box exposed in my underwear drawer the other day."

Julia giggled, touching his arm. "You just need to get this over with. Just do it."

"Hey, relax. It has to be the exact right time."

Shadow barreled inside ahead of me, as I asked them,

"right time for what?" Both my mom and Greg glanced at each other and turned crimson.

"What's going on?"

Greg quickly stepped forward, ushering me from the room. "Only trying to settle your mom's worries about her home repairs. I'm sure it won't be a fast process. How about a glass of wine?"

"We still have to board up the window and back door at her house. How about we go do that, and talk about evening dinner plans while we do?"

"You got it."

CHAPTER FIVE

By the time we sat down to eat dinner at a local diner, I had no more energy. We'd measured the window and door, bought plywood at Home Depot, and after a couple of hours getting things secured, we met up with the Lawsons. Actually cleaning Mom's house was a whole different animal for another day. She moved some necessary items to my house and worked with the insurance company to get a restoration company to come out the next day for the repair quote. Between the fire, smoke and water damage, it was an enormous undertaking.

While we waited for our food, I sat back in my chair listening to Greg's family telling my mother all about their view of the Superstition mountains. It was a great place. Greg had found a great deal on the land, with the gorgeous view of the infamous mountain range, several months prior when his company relocated him here on a job assignment. He also still owns a home in Northeastern Arizona in the small town of Heber, but couldn't pass up on the investment opportunity. Since his land purchase, he'd worked diligently to get a septic system installed and water and electric connected to the property. For now, he parked his enormous fifth-wheel trailer on the property, with the long-term plan to build his dream house someday. He sure sounded more comfortable moving to the big city now that he'd found this rural slice of heaven.

As I listened to them talk about everything RV, I recapitulated the past twenty-four hours. His family didn't seem all that bothered by being displaced because a dead woman was found in their rental unit. I couldn't stop thinking about what could have possibly happened to the poor woman. JJ had said they were waiting for tox screenings and the autopsy results. That reminded me that the homeowner, Melissa, mentioned the name of the victim: Carol Linton. Had mom's kitchen fire not happened, or had the alarm system not gone off at my business, I probably would have had time to do some research on the internet. *Who was the woman?* Melissa already ruled out her being a past tenant. *So how did the woman get into the house? Who are you, Carol Linton?*

"If you don't mind, Libby?"

My head whipped around to face Anne. "I'm so sorry. What was that?"

"Dana and I were saying that we'd be more than happy to help with the cooking." She leaned back while the server set a plate of food in front of her.

Despite wanting to be the consummate host, my brain

couldn't handle anything else today. The cheeseburger and fries that landed in front of me didn't even sound good right now.

"Yes, of course. But can we discuss those plans later?"

"Sure, no problem," Anne said, before she turned to her daughter and asked for the ketchup.

My mom patted my leg and whispered to me, "I'm so sorry, Libby."

I leaned close to her ear. "Everything will turn out fine. Don't you worry, we won't let these things stop us from having a wonderful Thanksgiving with our friends and family." I gave her the best confident smile I could muster.

As I bit into my juicy cheeseburger, I overheard Larry telling Greg and his father all the plans he had for the family while they were in Arizona. I wasn't sure how'd they find the time, but he was still rattling off things like hiking, kayaking, visiting the ghost town, and possibly making a run down to Tucson to go to the air museum and also get a tour of the old missile silo.

"Anyone else wanna go?" Larry asked, with his mouth full, looking around the table for a taker.

I managed to keep quiet, only able to think about all the work ahead of me. I barely heard how Greg responded, but it sounded as though they were making plans. Maybe that would help? Get all the extra people out of the house while I help Mom.

After getting my mom settled into her room for the night, I decided a glass of wine would help me calm my nerves. I poured a glass and joined Greg and Shadow in the backyard.

"Are you going hiking tomorrow?"

"No, hon. There's way too much to get done around

here." He reached out and took my free hand. "Are you sure we should host a large group for Thanksgiving? I think everyone would understand, given everything that's happened."

I sat down on the patio sofa and Shadow crawled up next to me. It'd been a long day and she'd been cooped up at home, which was unusual for us. Generally, she was with me most days at work. I considered what Greg proposed as I savored my first sip of merlot.

"It's Thanksgiving though. And your family has come a long way. I'd feel rotten not going through with our plans."

He sat down on the other side of us and put his hand on my knee. "I understand. I am worried you're taking on too much, though. Even if we downsized the event to be only my family…"

Greg understood the solemnness that swept across my face. How was I supposed to leave out *my* family, my dear friends, and those who have nowhere else to go for the holiday? I couldn't imagine that, so I plastered on a smile and turned to him. "I'll be fine. Tomorrow, everything will look brighter." I leaned over and gave him a kiss.

* * *

Shadow was the first to rouse the household. Her barking pierced the peaceful pre-dawn morning, and I bolted out of bed understanding the urgency in her voice.

"What is it, girl?"

I let her out of her crate, and she bolted to the back sliding glass door. Jumping intently at the glass and nearly clearing its six-foot height, I scolded her. "Shadow, down!" I reached for the lock and realized it wasn't in the locked position. As I slid it open, she scrambled to get through the doorway, down the steps from the elevated patio, and sprinted across the small yard to the side gate.

"Shadow!" I yelled after her.

Greg poked his head from the doorway. "What's wrong?"

"I'm not sure." I shouted and took off after her, finding the side gate wide open. "She got out!" I screamed back to Greg.

Neither of us had shoes on, but that didn't matter to me. I sprinted. In the distance, I saw her black figure running away from me and toward the end of the block.

"Shadow!" I screamed again.

My feet pounded against the asphalt, each step a jarring impact on my bare soles. I gasped for breath, racing after her, terrified she'd soon reach the traffic-filled intersection. I rounded the corner, frantically looking both directions. Seeing her now running down the next street, but away from where the traffic would be of concern, I slowed slightly for a second.

That's when I saw a man sprinting away, his legs churning with a frantic energy. He glanced over his shoulder, then made a sharp turn and disappeared from view.

"Shadow!" I shouted even louder, hearing a vehicle approaching from behind. I glanced and saw it was Greg in his white Tundra.

He slowed, and I jumped into the passenger seat. "She's … chasing … someone. Turn here!" I pointed to where I last saw my dog and the man.

Tires squealed as he rounded the corner far too fast for a residential neighborhood.

"Stop!" I screamed.

Both of us grunted when our seatbelts grasped tightly at our collarbones as our bodies lurched forward. I unlatched my belt, swung open the door, and jumped out. Shadow was limping slowly toward us. My eyes scanned the area; no one was around. I kneeled down and took Shadow into my arms.

"What happened?" I cooed, as I inspected her for an injury. "Can you drive down the block farther? Look for a guy—bright yellow trainers. Wearing all black."

Greg nodded and he was off.

I felt down each of Shadow's legs, carefully lifting each paw and watching for her reaction. Her paws were hot, but there was no obvious sign of injury. Not wanting her to take off running again, I encouraged her to lie down, waiting for Greg to come back. I stayed next to her, holding her collar tight, and continued looking for injuries.

The Tundra came into sight and Shadow abruptly stood.

"It's okay, sweetie. That's Greg. He's going to give us a ride home."

He asked if she was okay as he hurried around and opened the back door. She jumped right in without issue. We both shrugged. "I guess so."

Back at home, I winced, stepping down out of the truck and realizing how raw my feet were. I hobbled into the house and straight to the kitchen table, where I took a seat.

"I can't believe you ran all that way with nothing on your feet."

"I didn't even notice, honestly. Until now!"

"We have Epsom salts—want me to run you a bath?"

I nodded as I gently turned my left foot over to see the

damage. It was red, but no cuts. I switched feet and saw the blood on the right foot. "Oh boy. This one is going to be a problem."

Greg kneeled down to get a closer look. "Okay. Let's get it cleaned up and bandaged. You'll be okay."

Mom walked into the kitchen. "What was Shadow carrying on about?" Then she noticed Greg helping me up and guiding me as I hopped on one foot down the hallway. "What happened?"

Greg calmly told her he'd fill her in later, after I'd had a bath and got my wounds cleaned. "How about some coffee, Julia? Can you get that going?"

She nodded and quickly went into action.

While soaking in the warm water, I smelled bacon cooking and my stomach rumbled. I got out, dried off, and found my mom and Greg in the kitchen making breakfast. While we ate, Mom asked us if Shadow always woke us up with such gusto. We assured her it was not normal.

I remembered something. "The back door was unlocked when I took her out this morning. We must have been careless when we went to bed last night."

"Oh, that's not good. And even more so, we must have left the side gate opened too," Greg pointed out. "You've always had a lock on that gate, right? I went out there and looked all over. No lock anywhere. I checked to see if we'd set it up on the block fence—nope. Nowhere in the side yard either; I looked in the gravel all along the path leading to the front yard—didn't find it."

My eyes widened. *Had I really become that careless?* After several incidents in nearby neighborhoods over the past couple years, I thought I'd been more than diligent. Overall, we lived in a friendly neighborhood, but hearing the evening news, crime seemed to move closer and closer.

Mom added, "And you are always on me to make sure my place is all locked up… sheesh."

Ignoring the snipe from Mom, I turned back to Greg. "I never asked if you saw the man that ran from Shadow. Did you catch up to him?"

He shook his head.

Feeling defeated and worried, I slumped in the chair and took a sip of my coffee. "He was too far away to get any real detail, but I don't think that I recognize him from the neighborhood. His body type or anything. Shadow and I run these streets all the time, and I know he's not a runner I've seen before."

"Do you suppose Shadow chased after him because he was jogging through the neighborhood?" my mom asked us.

"She never has before. Then again, she's always on a leash. But why the alarming bark at our back door? And then for her to bolt around the side of the house like that. It makes me think the person was actually in our backyard. She's smart, and I think she followed his scent the second she got out of the house."

Greg nodded. "There's no way for us to know when someone opened that gate, but since she was outside last night with you, my guess is that it happened this morning. So you're probably right—Shadow heard the intruder and alerted us."

I sipped my coffee, trying to ignore my throbbing foot propped up on the chair next to me. How inconvenient, considering how much I needed to be on my feet in the upcoming week.

CHAPTER SIX

Quiet contemplation over coffee turned into our longest day yet.

After Greg doctored my right foot with an antibacterial ointment and a self-adhesive wrapping around the sole of my foot, I managed to get into my trainers and walk somewhat normally. There was a little hobble, but it felt much better.

Anne and Bill Lawson called Greg, asking for a ride over to a rental car company. Since they were no longer staying with their kids, they preferred having an additional car.

Mom and I met with the restoration company over at her house. That's when we learned her stay with us would not end anytime soon and the prognosis on the repairs was far worse than I'd imagined. The water damage sustained from the fire hoses basically required several new walls, new roofing, of course, a whole new kitchen, but it even extended into the living room flooring and walls. Insurance would cover it, so that was the good news. However, they informed us it could take a few months to complete.

My mom took that news the hardest. I saw the color drain from her face when she realized the full extent. We had a lot of work ahead of us. They confirmed they would clear out all the damaged and destroyed items, and they had companies they'd hire to clean and preserve the furniture that could be salvaged from the smoke damage. But it was up to us to remove undamaged personal effects before they began. Smoke damage had made its way throughout the house, far worse than what we'd initially realized. They explained that commonly happens when smoke makes its way through the ventilation system. All linens, carpeting, window coverings, had a tinge of black to them and smelled of smoke. Professional cleaning would be necessary for everything we wanted to keep.

Items enclosed in the rooms farthest away from the fire, such as within dresser drawers, we'd have to go through and put into storage until all the repairs were completed. My eyes darted around the guest room, then her room, and her hobby room. There was so much to go through. I looked over at my mom and saw her look of despair. The man explaining the process must have picked up on that as well.

"Hey, the good news is that you have time." He smiled, trying for optimism. "Due to the upcoming holiday, we won't be able to start for a few weeks."

I reached out when I thought my mom's legs were

going to give out. It's rare to see my mother cry, but I saw her tears brimming. Nudging her and whispering, I told her, "It's okay. We have Thanksgiving—then after that, we'll tackle each thing one at a time. That gives us a little time." I realized then I was trying to convince myself of this as much as anyone.

Soon after we'd signed the paperwork and the restoration people had left, Lexi called.

"Hey you! Are you on your way here?" she asked.

"No. I don't have appointments today. Kind of have my hands full at the moment."

"Oh? Well, Melissa Barnstead is here."

I groaned. "I told Cody to book her with someone else." My patience was running thin.

"She insists."

"Lexi, I can't … I don't have time to go into everything now, but my mom's house caught fire, someone tried to break into mine, and we're supposed to be hosting *many* people in mere days. I really need someone else to take the appointment. Please."

"Oh jeez. And after Greg's family finding a dead body. What next? Is your mom okay?"

I chuckled. "Yes. She's fine, but her house is not."

"Isn't that where we were going to cook?"

"*Were* being the operative word, yes. Look, I'll catch you up on everything shortly. For now, help me with Melissa and call me later?"

"No problem, my friend. Hey, are *you* okay?"

I squelched the catch in my throat. "I'll be fine."

Mom followed me in her car back to my house. When we walked in, I read a note left by Greg saying he was with the family out at the trailer. He invited us to join them whenever we were able. Even though it wasn't even noon, I set the piece of paper down on the counter, thinking that all I wanted to do was to crawl back into bed.

My phone chimed, and I pulled it from my pocket. Bella's text read: Looking forward to seeing you! When are we cooking? Let me know the plan.

I shoved the phone back in my pocket and took Shadow outside. Quickly, I double-checked the side gate and saw that Greg had secured it again with a new lock. Bless him. Shadow sniffed all around and stood up against the block wall, trying to see over.

"Not a chance, girl."

She whined and continued sniffing the area intently. I stood, soaking in some sunshine while she did her business. My mind went back to the early morning hours. *Was Greg correct? Had that man been in our backyard?* I didn't doubt it based on Shadow's reaction. I just couldn't understand *why*.

Mom mulled over my lists, thumbing through the recipe books, when we walked back inside. Even though I'd rather not have to think about any of it, I knew it was best to stay busy. We plotted out the plan for pre-cooking some dishes, as well as how we'd handle the Thanksgiving Day rush, too. Hosting my first holiday meal trying to make a good impression on Greg's family—while also pleasing all the friends, too, I prayed it would all turn out perfectly.

Greg called and said they were headed out to the lake and would probably eat lunch there.

"Wanna take a break and come with us?"

"I would love to, but we're right in the thick of planning. You guys go have fun and we'll see you when you get back. Are you still thinking of going to Tucson tomorrow?"

"We'll see. They definitely want to stay busy—trying

not to think of the police investigation, I think."

"Understood. Yeah, you play tourist guide, and Mom and I will get ready for next week's big day."

"Wish it was different, and you were here with us, but completely understand. We'll be home soon."

* * *

Before Mom and I knew it, the whole afternoon had passed. The gang showed up, all sunburned and exhilarated from an afternoon playing at the lake.

"You should have seen it, Aunt Libby," Joey's brown eyes bulged with excitement. He pushed his round-shaped glasses up from where they slipped on his nose. "I found a *huge* lizard. Mom wouldn't let me keep him, but she did let me bring back several bugs. Wanna see?"

My eyes scanned quickly, looking for bugs. *Where are they?* I tentatively gave a "uh, huh…" and he ran out the front door.

"Sorry Libby, he's obsessed with creepy crawlies. I asked him to leave them outside. Are you sure you want him to bring them inside?" Dana asked.

It was too late. Joey, who I found myself comparing to a miniature Harry Potter, ran up to us, plopped himself down on the floor, and opened up a small plastic contraption. Out popped an enormous furry spider.

"*What* is THAT?" I screamed and jumped up on the couch.

His sister, Lila, screeched and ran from the room.

Joey's eyes lit up, his wide smile beaming. "It's a tarantula!"

All conversation ceased, and every adult scanned the

floor; all eyes searching for the spider.

Dana was shockingly calm. "Joey, where did it go?"

He shrugged. "Don't worry, he'll come back. He likes me."

Greg's eyes met mine with an *are you kidding me?* expression. He immediately went into a save-the-day mode, seeking the spider.

"Anne, would you like to go outside with me?" my mom asked.

She didn't have to be asked twice. They raced out the door.

As I stood on my sofa, watching the scene unfold, I had a sinking feeling. "Um, Joey … what else was in that, er, that carrier?"

"Oh, just several bugs Terry likes to eat."

"Terry?"

"The tarantula!"

"Ok, ok," my heart thumped. "What *type* of bugs?"

"Some stink bugs, a millipede, and I even found a scorpion—sooo cool!"

"*What*?!" I looked at Dana for confirmation.

She was nodding. "He didn't pick them up, don't worry."

"That's not what concerns me! Look at the cage— they're gone, too!"

Lila peeked around the corner from the hallway. "You're so stupid, Joey! Now they're going to eat all of us!" She ran out the front door screaming, looking for her grandmother.

"I'm outta here, too." I leaped off the sofa, and in a tip-toe run, I bolted for the front door. "Greg, Dana, *find them*!" I yelled before slamming the front door.

I found Mom, Anne, and Lila out at the street curb. "It's official. There's no way I can handle having kids," I declared. "Especially boys."

They laughed, but didn't disagree with me.

It wasn't long before the guys came outside, with the critters recaptured inside the bug container. Dana promised Joey would keep his critters outside. Lila slugged her brother in the arm.

"Shall we do something about dinner?" I asked.

We settled on a Mexican food restaurant nearby, and afterward they'd head back to the trailer and hotel, respectively.

Hours later, as Greg and I lay in bed, I asked, "Did you play with bugs as a small boy?"

"Probably. You didn't?"

"No!"

"But you love the outdoors?"

"Yes, I do. And I respect the wildlife enough to leave them alone." I smiled, leaning over and giving him a kiss.

"I think we're getting up and taking a hike in the morning. Wanna come?"

"I'll answer that after a good night's sleep. I think so, but what a day it's been."

The tarantula had been a fleeting encounter, yet its image lingered in my mind as I tried falling asleep. Trying to quiet the thoughts in my head, the ever-present spider image seemed to grow larger, its menacing fangs and hairy legs magnified in the dark presence behind my eyelids.

Each creak in the house, each shadow cast by the moonlight, seemed to be a potential threat. I tossed and turned, my body restless, my mind unable to relax. As the hours ticked by, I went from feeling my skin crawl to squirming when my foot throbbed to visually adding more tasks to the list. It felt as though I was awake all night long.

* * *

I woke the next morning finding a note on the empty pillow next to mine.

I didn't want to wake you—you were sound asleep. I'm joining the family for hiking; call me when you're up.

Stretching, I glanced at the clock. *Eight?* I couldn't remember the last time I slept that late. Then I remembered how late it was before I'd finally drifted off. It was tempting to stay in bed. Instead, I hopped out, still hobbling and pampering my injured foot, but made my way to the kitchen for coffee. Mom was at the kitchen table.

"Did Greg take Shadow?"

She nodded, turning the page on her newspaper.

"You actually still get the newspaper?"

"I do—I'm having it forwarded here for now until I get back in my house."

"That's cool."

I popped a K-cup into the machine to brew. Sitting down next to Mom, I grabbed a section and began reading. I could honestly say that I'd never read my news in this manner. I'd never subscribed to the local paper in my adult life—I mean, why? My phone delivered all the news I could digest, anyway.

"Are you going hiking, too?" Mom asked.

"Um, not sure. I assume they've already left, but I suppose I should call, shouldn't I?" I took a sip of coffee and shrugged, rethinking that. "You know, it's probably best I don't push it with my injured foot. Plus, this is really nice." I stared out the back door, listening to the silence in the room. "Maybe a nice quiet morning is more what I need right now—like the calm before the storm?"

"True, we're going to be busy for days."

I savored a few more sips of coffee before checking my phone. That's when my nice, peaceful morning ended.

The text read: Call me ASAP. Larry's missing.

CHAPTER SEVEN

Unable to reach Greg by phone, my mom and I drove out to Apache Junction, where his family was staying. As I pulled up, my heart sank. We parked off to the side at the end of the dirt road, near two police cruisers. As soon as I stepped out, Shadow let off a loud bark and ran straight for me. I hobbled along and Mom stuck by my side. And that's when I saw him; JJ was there. *Why were police officers and a detective talking to the Lawsons?*

Greg's fingers ran through his thick brown hair. His face etched with worry lines. The usual brilliant smile was now a straight sealed-lip grimace. Although I was tempted to check in with JJ first, I walked right over to Greg. The detective was in deep conversation with an officer, anyway; I was sure he wouldn't appreciate me interrupting.

"What happened?" I asked Greg.

"Larry. He went hiking last night, apparently. No one has seen him since."

"Last night?" I questioned. "Okay. Well, he is a grown adult. And from what I remember, he's also famous for setting off without telling anyone." Memories from our Northern New Mexico trip came flooding back. Larry went missing then, too.

"You're right, it isn't abnormal for him. But this is…" he held up a plastic bag which contained a phone, a scrap of material, and a shoe. "A hiker turned these in at the Lost Dutchman State Park. Apparently, they found these along the trail early this morning."

"And I guess you've validated the phone is his…"

"The police called a couple of his contacts, ultimately reaching my mom. Dad then called me … and here we are."

"Is that flannel?"

Greg nodded. "Dana says this could be the shirt he was wearing yesterday. She wasn't entirely certain, but he has several flannel shirts."

JJ walked up. "Libby—have you talked to Lexi this morning?"

I shook my head.

"You're going to want to call her. I guess the massage with Melissa …" he stopped when an officer yelled out to him.

"JJ—we've got something. C'mon!"

He ran off, and I pulled my phone out, dialing my friend. As I walked away from the group, I saw Bill pulling Anne closer to him. Dana stepped out from the trailer, interested in the commotion.

"Lexi—hi," I started.

"Libby. How well do you know the Barnsteads?"

"Why?"

"I know they've been clients since we first opened, but I learned things today that could put them at the top of the suspect list in that woman's death."

Stunned, all I could get out was, "What?"

"Yes. I had to tell JJ—I'm sorry."

"What for? Of course, if there's something that ties them to the case, he has to know. What was it?"

"Where are you?"

"Out at Greg's. JJ is here too ... well, *was* here. He and the other officers just tore off. I guess they're concerned something's happened to Larry."

"What happened to Larry?"

"He went hiking ... hey, let me finish up here, and then I'll meet you at the office. We've got to catch up. I need to know how the Barnsteads are involved."

"See you soon."

Dana motioned me to the trailer, and I followed her inside. Her kids were in the bunk beds in the back, with headsets on their ears, fixated on playing a video game.

"What's all this business about Larry gone missing?" I asked.

"I don't know why this family does this every single time he ventures out—they're helicopter parents, for sure. He's a grown-ass adult. Sheesh!"

I chuckled, nodding my head. I couldn't disagree with that. "Did you hear they found some items of his?"

"No. Well, they asked me something about the shirt he was wearing when he left yesterday. Honestly, I've stayed in here, tuning my parents out. I'm so sick of them constantly worried about Larry. He went out hiking to watch the sunset—we went to bed early. I felt exhausted after yesterday at the lake. I never even noticed he hadn't returned."

"Yeah, they found part of his shirt … a shoe? And, of course, his phone. That's how the authorities reached your parents."

"Interesting. He didn't have it password protected."

I looked at her questioningly. "I was actually more concerned about the shoe. Can't hike very far without proper footwear." The bottom of my foot throbbed as I said it aloud.

"Yeah, true. Hadn't thought of that. Wanna Coke?"

I shook my head. "I've gotta head back to town shortly. Mom and I have worked out the plan. We'll get together to meal prep, cooking ahead so that Thanksgiving Day isn't so much. But don't worry—not until after this weekend. We have plenty of time next week."

"Great, let me know when and where, and I'll be happy to get away from this bunch. I'm still hoping we're going to Tucson later. Surely Larry will show up."

"Yeah, I know you all want to get touristy stuff in while you're here. Speaking of which, your husband … when does Joe arrive?"

"Most likely, the evening before Thanksgiving. Maybe even the morning of … and then he's flies right back out the next day. It's the busiest time of year for the airlines." She rolled her eyes. "I can't remember the last time we all spent an entire holiday weekend together. You'd think with tenure, he'd start getting some of these holidays off."

I sympathized with her, but then excused myself,

reminding her I needed to leave soon. When I stepped outside, Greg and my mom approached. I took his hand and asked to talk to him. Mom joined Dana in the trailer.

"How serious is this? Isn't it possible Larry is simply exploring and will return soon?"

"Normally, I'd agree with you. However, Larry is super attached to that phone—it's his livelihood. Also, how far would he be able to hike with only one shoe?"

"Yeah, I was wondering about that, too. Do you know why JJ was called in for this one?"

"I'm not entirely sure. But I know Officer Brown, and I'm thankful they're taking it seriously. Normally, they don't consider an adult missing until after forty-eight hours." He looked around to ensure that nobody was overhearing him. "Plus, there's something they aren't saying. I can feel it— and that's probably why JJ was called in."

"Listen, I've gotta stop by work. Is it okay if Mom hangs here with all of you?"

"Sure. I meant to ask last night before the great spider escape, but how'd it go with the insurance company?"

"That's a long story, but the shortened version … Mom will be with us for a while."

"How long is a while?"

"Several months."

He didn't grimace, but only pulled me into a hug. That's another reason why I loved this man.

CHAPTER EIGHT

I pulled up into the spa parking lot and saw it was quite packed, for the Saturday before Thanksgiving. Shadow hopped down from the back seat when I opened the back door and we headed inside. Cody smiled at us, pointing at his earbud as he spoke to a customer over the phone. I waved and pushed through the glass doors beyond the front counter.

Several customers sat in our Serenity Room. I gave a slight tug to Shadow's leash, and she responded perfectly, leaving the customers alone. We walked ahead to the second set of doors and disappeared into the rear of the building. As soon as I unleashed her, she ran to Lexi, whom we found sitting at her desk. She already had a treat out and instructed Shadow's wriggling body to sit. As soon as she did, Lexi then told her to lie down. On that command, Shadow received her treat. It truly took a village to raise this one-year-old pup—especially one who was continuing to work on her search and rescue training skills.

"I've missed you two!" Lexi stood, came around the desk and gave me a gigantic hug. "We keep passing in the night, I guess."

I chuckled. "It's been quite the time, that's for sure."

She asked me about Greg's family. Leaving out details of Larry's hike, I provided the latest update on who was staying where and how it'd gone so far since their discovery of the dead body. I used to always assume she got information from JJ, but learned that's not how it worked with law enforcement families. They rarely talked about cases. He told me once he tried hard to keep his work out of his home.

Her kind eyes softened. "And how's your mom doing? I can't imagine being displaced … and at the holidays."

I ran through everything we knew from the insurance and restoration companies. There was still so much more to do, but for now, I couldn't allow myself to get too bogged down by it all.

"You said something over the phone about a conversation with Melissa?" I prompted Lexi.

"Yes! Omigod. That family…"

My brows furrowed, encouraging her to go on.

"I think Fred has a whole side gig going on that could definitely drag them into that murder investigation."

"What do you mean?"

She detailed the bits and pieces she'd put together from Melissa's table top confession. That's the term we've come to call the crazy things clients tell us during massage sessions. From this one, she gathered Melissa was afraid investigators would uncover just how many properties they owned throughout the valley. Actually, throughout the world.

"I didn't know they were *that* wealthy?" I noted.

"Exactly. Apparently, the casualness we see has to be a smokescreen."

"And they make all their money through real estate?"

"Well, that's where I might be allowing my imagination to run wild—I honestly don't know—but gauging from some of her comments, and from the places they continue to buy properties, I wondered whether they are part of some foreign investment scheme."

"What makes you say that? Did Melissa tell you they are?"

"No. She stopped short of detailing exactly how they made their money. Actually, by the end of the session, I got the distinct feeling that she realized she'd said too much."

"What exactly did she say?"

Lexi told the story of how they bought their place in Mexico. Since it was so foreign to anything the Johnsons had ever done, she asked how one goes about buying property in foreign countries—how would a mortgage work, for instance? Casually, Melissa let it slip that the Mexico property and one in the Bahamas were cash purchases. They needed to spend cash to save them from being taxed.

"I suppose that's what the rich do ... but how is that related to some 'side gig' which could relate to the murder?"

"Sure. Real estate can be a perfectly lucrative and legal investment—but I kept picking up on her description of what I interpreted to mean 'to hide cash'. But it wasn't this part that was concerning. It was her worry over the authorities finding out about their *illegally hired help*."

"Oh, no."

"Why would she tell me about that? I don't know. Does she not know that my husband is JJ, the absolute *play-by-the-book* of all detectives? Maybe she doesn't."

I giggled when she used her air quotes describing my law enforcement friend so well. "So, hired help ... would that be the cleaning crews for their rentals?"

"I can only guess, but perhaps. They have over fifty properties they rent out—and that's only here in Arizona."

"Whoa, I did not know they owned *that* many. And all of it online vacation rental business?"

"I'm not sure. Some could be long-term rentals, I don't know. But throughout the world they invest, she said, in *thousands* of properties."

"That they own themselves? No wonder they don't want to be taxed on all that income!"

"At one point during the conversation, she made a remark about 'when they find out'. I asked for clarification, because I thought she related that to the dead body on the property here. That's when she tensed and probably realized she'd already told me *way* too much. She changed subjects and their business never came up again."

"So, you've told JJ all this, right? It could mean whoever *they* are, well, they could be involved in what happened at their rental unit."

"I know! I'll talk to him tonight. Since he left the house this morning, I haven't had a chance. When I tried calling, it went straight to voice mail."

"Ah, yeah. He's with the Lawsons and law enforcement over at Greg's property."

"Why?"

"Apparently, Larry went hiking after dinner last night and no one has seen him since."

She looked skeptical and asked, "Why do they need law enforcement? Has he even been gone long enough to be considered missing?"

"Exactly what I asked too, and I'm not sure. Hopefully, we'll learn more later."

Changing subjects, she smiled. "Hey, when are we getting together for cooking?" Her smile faded; the situation dawning on her. "Oh shoot, we were going to do that at Julia's, weren't we?"

I nodded. "Mom and I have a Plan B in mind now. Starting Monday, we'll start prepping pies and then the side dishes—a few things each day. You know, the stuff that can be prepared or baked a few days early. Then, on Wednesday evening, we'll assign different households to heat the already prepped dishes on Thursday, bringing them over to my house that day. That way, my oven is free for the turkey and I can actually visit with the guests instead of being stuck in the kitchen."

"Sounds perfect. In fact, you could probably just ask each household to create something—you know, potluck style."

"I know. I'm still stuck on mostly preparing this as a group effort—that was supposed to be the 'fun part' about it. You know, for everyone to be together and get to know one another. And, similar to potluck style, we are counting on using diverse family recipes, but I really want it to be an experience and collaborative effort."

Her eyes shone as she displayed a brilliant smile. "Oh! You want to impress your future in-laws! I understand now…" she ribbed.

"No! That's not it." The flush warmed its way over my face and I couldn't hold back from laughing. "Ok, I will admit that I want the Lawsons to feel welcome among my group of friends—after all, you all *are* my family. And that would hold true no matter how long Greg and I are together. In-laws? No one is talking about marriage yet, Lexi!"

Her side-eyed glance and the curl to her upper lip made me wonder if she knew something I didn't. My stomach clenched at the same time as I felt a tingling creep through my body. I couldn't think about that. I had work to do.

My phone chimed as I walked through the spa, looking for my dog so we could go. I glanced at the display and saw a text message from my mom. Greg was driving her back to the house, and she wondered where I was. I quickly texted I would meet them there. That reminded me: there was another errand to run later. Mom still needed a key to our house.

I pulled up and saw Greg's Tundra already in the driveway. Shadow jumped out of my vehicle and ran to the front door. By the time I caught up to her, I saw she'd barreled on through the open door. And that's right where I found Greg and Julia staring over a chaotic scene.

CHAPTER NINE

There was no mistaking what happened. The room was a testament to the absolute devastation wrought by thieves. The once-tidy living room and kitchen area was now a jumble of overturned furniture and scattered belongings. Some kitchen cabinet doors dangled precariously by one hinge. Glassware, pots and pans, and dishes were strewn everywhere. Broken glass from the shattered back sliding door littered the ground, casting sparkles across the tile floor from the incoming beams of sunlight.

Greg took me in his arms. "It's okay. We'll get it cleaned up. I already grabbed Shadow and ushered her into the garage for now—you know, all this glass."

I wrangled away from his grasp, turning down the hallway, and looking into each room. The same destruction was everywhere. My eyes cast over the contents of the dresser drawers strewn across the floor. The closet doors hung open, their shelves emptied. Feeling utterly violated, I stepped out of my bedroom, ran down the hallway, and directly out the front door. Nausea washed over me like a churning ocean within, a sickening feeling threatening to rise. My head throbbed; my vision blurred slightly. Weak and lightheaded, bending forward, I fought to keep my composure.

I felt my mom's quiet presence a second before her hand found my shoulder. "It'll be okay, Libby," she said soothingly, rubbing my back.

I closed my eyes once more. *How was anything going to be okay? Why were all these things happening? Why us?* I sank down to the ground, supporting my back against the front of the house.

"Did you guys call the police?" I asked, looking up at her solemnly.

"Yes. They're on their way."

By the time the police left a couple of hours later, Greg had been on the phone with his parents—Larry had still not shown up. There was talk of forming a search and rescue, of which Greg was steering the conversation. But first, he measured and ran to Home Depot for more plywood, this time to seal up the back of my home.

Lexi and Bella had come over to help us. My sister Jordan offered, but she'd have brought the kids with her and I thought that'd be too much. We put all the living room furniture back into its proper position again. We swept and vacuumed the glass from the flooring and furniture, but regardless, I still advised everyone to wear shoes due to randomly finding more shards of glass. So many dishes were smashed beyond repair, but we put what we could back into the cabinets.

Bella's voice broke through the stupor I'd been in, focusing on what to salvage or what to throw away. "Do you know what this is?" She held up what looked to be a dingy gray cloth.

"No idea. Looks good enough to dust with, though. Keep it." I pointed to a 'keep pile' across the room and she tossed it on top.

Later, long past dinnertime, I sat back on the couch, simply exhausted. I watched Greg from across the room talking on his phone, organizing people, and remaining so calm. *How was he so good at this?* Quiet, steady, gentle, and unshaken. He never got rattled. I'd been out of my mind all afternoon—from seeing the destruction, to dealing with the police *again*, to cleaning and trying not to scream.

The toughest part had been going through the contents and trying to figure out what the thieves had taken. They stole the obvious—all the electronics throughout the house, which consisted of two televisions, our Echo, several clocks (which surprised me), Greg's laptop (mine was at work), and the microwave and air fryer. The bedroom content was more difficult to pinpoint. They seemed to have rummaged through the dresser drawers in search of valuable items, but they would be sorely disappointed. I know jewelry was missing, but I had nothing of value—it was mostly costume or inexpensive pieces.

Thankfully, Greg had not moved much into my home yet since his stay was initially meant to be temporary. He simply hadn't had time with his summer in Alaska for SAR training. When we inspected the garage, boxes of his belongings still lined the walls, and it hadn't appeared the thieves had even gone in there. We were grateful for that.

His voice startled me when I realized he'd finished on the phone. "The family already picked up some food for dinner. They don't want to leave the trailer in case Larry comes home."

I nodded and scooted over so he could sit down next to me.

"Why don't I take you ladies out for dinner?" We both looked around the room, realizing it was a mess. Better than before, but still in need of a deep cleaning.

Lexi overheard and suggested instead that we all go to her house—that way we could bring Shadow, too. She also understood being in public right now would not be comfortable for me, and I loved my friend for her empathy.

After freshening up and putting on clean clothing, we loaded into Greg's truck and headed over the few miles to our friend's house. Bella bowed out; she had plans with Cody and Brad.

Joshua and JJ greeted us in the kitchen, where they'd already received the delivered pizzas. He pulled me aside and asked about the break-in, telling me how sorry he was I had to deal with yet one more thing. While I had his attention momentarily, I told him about the man Shadow chased through our neighborhood. It'd been weighing on me, and with so many other things happening, I hadn't brought it back up with Greg.

"I don't have a great description of him, but I think there is a connection. Our gate lock was missing, and the gate left open. *Something* alerted Shadow."

He made a mental note and mentioned he'd speak to the officers in charge.

Lexi called us over; she already pulled plates from the

cabinets and set them out. She found utensils and tossed the two large salads with them, then turned to find dressing in the refrigerator.

"Go ahead and dig in," she turned around to say.

Joshua, their five-year-old, hopped up and down, trying to see over the countertop. "Is there pepperoni?" I lifted him up so he could point out his favorite kind, and then helped him fill his plate and get it to the table without spilling.

JJ had already set out silverware on the large round dinner table, and now he pulled wine and beer from the refrigerator. "Take your pick. Or, of course, we have water too." He grabbed the carton of milk and poured a small glass for his son.

Once everyone took their seats, they all directed their attention toward eating. Even Joshua was quiet. Prior to smelling the pizza aroma, I hadn't felt hungry at all. In fact, nausea was the predominate sensation I'd felt all afternoon. But I had to admit now picking at my salad that food was exactly what I needed.

As soon as Joshua finished, he and Shadow ran upstairs to his playroom. Lexi had been waiting for that moment. She launched right in with her story about Melissa's tabletop confession from earlier in the day. I saw her energy deflate when JJ acknowledged his team had already discovered their holding companies and offshore accounts. They asked the Barnsteads to remain in Arizona for the time being while their investigation continued.

"Now we're focusing on interviews with the Santos family."

"The property manager?" I asked.

He nodded. "It seems it might be a family affair. His

wife runs a cleaning business, and I believe her crew may have been the last people in the house. Well, at least after the last tenants, and prior to the Lawsons finding the dead body."

"What has the cleaning crew said? I mean, I'm sure they haven't said 'oh yeah, we left that lady's body in the bathtub,' but I imagine they are critical for establishing a timeline."

Everyone chuckled at the levity, but JJ was stone-cold serious in his reply. "Libby, I already see your wheels turning. Please leave this up to us to solve. And you know I can't give you much detail." He looked around the table as if to warn everyone there against the questions they were about to launch his direction.

I loved JJ dearly, but my goodness, he was infuriatingly by-the-book when it came to his investigations. I mean, what did he expect? That I was a threat to his job? No way! That is one job I'd never step into voluntarily. Ok, admittedly, I'm nosey. Always have been, probably always will be. But I would not want to make law enforcement my profession. In fact, one could argue that tabletop confessions at the spa were a much better way to satisfy my inquisitive nature.

Greg changed subjects by giving an update about the search and rescue for Larry. As soon as I heard Shadow's name involved, I tuned into their discussion.

"Had we not found those personal effects, I think it would definitely be a situation of a man who was simply overdue back from his hike. The mountains are treacherous, though, and we need to ensure that he hasn't been injured and unable to return on his own."

JJ finished his beer. "True. It might be different if

he were a known local man who frequently explores the area—there are plenty of them that go out days at a time. But Larry's not from here and has no experience in those hills."

I wanted to find out why he was involved, but after my last scolding, I chose to sit back and listen, hoping he'd divulge that on his own. Instead, Lexi boldly claimed that she thought Larry was just off 'being Larry' again.

Greg nodded. "You and I both. At least initially, but somehow, this time around it seems a little different to me. You're right, my brother is an adventurer and rarely sits still. The man is constantly on the go, and with that, *always* motivated by a pretty woman. That said, the family's stated he legitimately sounded as though he just wanted to get some exercise. To my knowledge, there wasn't anyone he met—like a pretty Arizona lady—that he potentially ran off with."

I remembered back in Taos, the winter prior, how a group of pretty women had lured him away from the wedding festivities. He had partied way too hard, disappearing for days. And, I agreed with Greg; I hadn't noticed him flirting with anyone since they'd arrived here in Arizona this trip. Then, I remembered something else.

"The first night they arrived—after all that drama at the rental—we still don't know where he ran off to, right?"

Greg stared at me for a second. It was only then that I got the idea he hadn't wanted all that mentioned again.

JJ waited patiently.

Greg finished his beer, then stood and asked JJ, "Want another one while I'm up?"

JJ nodded.

Greg grabbed the beers, placing one in front of JJ. As

he opened his, he cleared his throat. "That's right. I'm not sure where he went off to that night. For all we know, he was outside looking at stars while we all slept. Doesn't much matter now. My sense this time around is that he could be in some trouble. Like I mentioned, those mountains have taken many lives. I want to be sure his isn't one of them."

"Of course."

JJ was mulling something in his mind. "Did your parents confirm that shoe was his?"

"Pretty sure, yeah," Greg nodded.

"He headed out on a long hike with trainers on? Wouldn't an experienced outdoors enthusiast wear his hiking boots?"

Greg nodded again. "If he had planned on a hiking trip when he packed? Sure."

My eyelids were heavy and the evening's conversation was even more burdensome. Lexi reached out and patted my hand. Signaling to Greg, she said, "This one needs her sleep."

CHAPTER TEN

Sunday morning, and after a solid eight hours of sleep, I got up with Shadow. Our back door exit, now having been sealed off by plywood, I attached her harness and leash and we headed out the front door for a walk.

The morning was cool, a much-appreciated relief from our brutal summer heat. Fall in Arizona was always my favorite. Few people were out this early, which also made it my favorite time of day—six o'clock. As we walked along at a brisk clip, I started processing another to-do list in my mind. Greg and Shadow were leaving for the search job soon, so I'd pack a lunch and make sure Shadow had her provisions as well. After they left, I needed to finish cleaning the house—more vacuuming, dusting, steaming the tile floors, and washing all the linens. I would have to take stock of the dishes that had made it through the melee, and I prayed shopping for new ones wouldn't be a required task for this week on top of everything else.

We turned the last corner before arriving back at my house. Greg was already loading his Tundra as we walked up. Shadow immediately jumped into the vehicle.

Giving Greg a kiss, I said, "Looks like someone is ready to go."

He chuckled and then directed his answer to Shadow. "Yeah, not quite yet, sweet girl. We've gotta go eat breakfast, so we'll be strong for this hike." He coaxed her out and we went inside the house.

"Mom's not up yet?" I noted quietly.

"I think all this has taken its toll on everyone."

I made coffee and Greg found the eggs, sausage, and bread. Soon, we had a full breakfast before us and a sleepy-looking Julia filed into the kitchen in her robe.

"Good morning!" I greeted.

"Is it?"

We had a role reversal this morning; mom was always cheerful, first thing when she woke. It always took at least one cup of coffee and my morning exercise before a smile emerged on my face.

"Well, there's coffee—so it can't be all that bad." I got up and poured her a cup, while she took a seat at the table.

"That pizza didn't sit quite right all night."

"It's hard to eat that late, isn't it?"

She nodded and then carefully sipped her black coffee.

Greg wiped his face, scooted his chair back, and took his dishes to the kitchen sink.

I pulled Shadow's food from a cabinet. "I'll get some food and treats for Shadow. Want me to fix you a few sandwiches or something?"

He came up behind me, squeezing my shoulders. "That'd be fantastic, sweetheart. I'm going to load up the extra gallons of water we've got in the garage and we'll need to pull out of here in about fifteen."

"Got it! Shadow will be ready."

Mom set her mug down, her eyes already had a tiny bit more sparkle in them. Shaking her head, she expressed disbelief, "I can't believe Larry might be hurt up on that mountain. What's going on in the universe this week?"

I pulled out six slices of multi-grain bread and laid them out in three pairs. Opening the peanut butter jar, I stuck the knife in, pulling out a large glob and started spreading it on one of the slices.

"Mom, I'm trying not to ask that question for fear of what may be next," I said, spreading the gooey brown protein on each of three slices, and then grabbing the jar of strawberry preserves.

"On the week where we're supposed to be so thankful. Where families gather for good—not all this *bad*."

"I understand, Mom. I feel the same. However, if there's one thing I have learned from you ... that is, no matter how bad it gets, someone in the world *always* has it worse. So we're going to be grateful for everything we *do have*." My eyes stung with tears. "You have a house—it just needs a little repair. I have a house with a few less things in it—thank you, thieves, for helping me clear some space. I'm not even sure how to be grateful for a dead woman, so I'll leave that one alone. But thank you, Lord, for helping Greg and Shadow find Larry safely. Please let everyone come home this afternoon safe and sound."

"Since when do you pray?" Mom asked.

"Oh, c'mon … just because I tend to believe more in the eastern philosophies, does not mean I'm opposed to prayer."

"Lexi is trying to get you to meditate all the time without success."

"I've had some success," I scoffed. "Anyway, that is not the point, Mother. My point was that *you* taught me all this. You are the optimistic, positive voice of our family. So, drink up that coffee and let's get on with fixing things. You've always taught me to stop complaining and to *do something*. Let's *do something*. We'll feel better." Tears were streaming down my face now.

Mom stood up and came over to put her arms around me. "You were paying attention, after all." We both sniffled, but had a good chuckle.

When Greg stepped into the room, he paused, seeing us crying. "What did I miss?"

I held up a bag with his sandwiches, a couple bags of chips, a few apples and some extra protein bars. "Nothing." I smiled sweetly.

He didn't buy it, but also didn't press.

We kissed and then they were off on their mission.

Hours later, the late morning sun filtered through the side windows, casting a warm glow throughout the room. Mom, wearing dark sweatpants and a t-shirt, squirted more of the lemon-scented floor cleaner and then methodically moved the steamer around the tiled floor.

I stayed ahead of her, vacuuming yet again, and making my way toward the entryway and hallway. Glancing at the clock, anxiety pricked at me. I turned off the vacuum when

I noticed my mother had also stopped. "Mom, are we sure we have enough room for everyone?"

She looked around, wiping her brow, and then we both found our eyes fixated on the ugly brown plywood that darkened the normally light-filled sliding glass door space.

"I was counting on having people outside as much as inside. It's going to be very cramped in here—especially when we set up the tables." I plopped down onto my recliner, which was temporarily moved near the breakfast bar.

Nothing normally rattled Julia Madsen, but I could see from her furrowed brow that we both were exhausted. "Maybe we should come up with a Plan C over lunch?"

She perked up with that suggestion and we put our cleaning devices aside for the moment. I opened the refrigerator and pulled out some sandwich makings, and, before long, we sat on the barstools, nourishing ourselves for the long workday ahead.

My phone chimed—it was my friend, Sage. She texted: what time are we gathering tomorrow for cooking?

I sighed, tired of this question, but also unrelenting in wanting to keep the plans we had in place. I decided it would be better to call and explain what was happening. After getting out all the initial bits about murder, theft, and fire … she was speechless.

"Libby, it's okay to cancel Thanksgiving this year. It sounds like you've got your hands full enough as it is."

"I know. Mom has said the same. However, I'm that stubborn one who wants to carry on. I mean, what more could possibly happen?"

My mom's head whipped around and she scowled at me.

"Careful, Libby," Sage said at the same time. "No time for tempting fate here. But I understand what you're saying. I'm sure the worst is behind you all now and we're going to have a beautiful meal later this week."

"That's my intention. Now, where to fit everyone in my home is going to be interesting, especially since the sliding door won't be replaced by Thursday. Anyway, I'm sure we'll come up with something, but the purpose of my call was just to fill you in and let you know we'll start with some meal prep around nine tomorrow morning. I have you, Cody and Brad, and Bella on the schedule for tomorrow to teach us how to make your favorite family recipes."

"Oh, this will be so much fun!" she squealed. "I've never done it like this—the way you're involving everyone and creating these little, oh, what do you call it … like cooking workshops. That's so cool! How interactive and fun."

I tried to remain excited because a week ago I had thought the idea was super cool. Right now, I was close to implementing a Plan C, meaning scrapping the whole idea and returning to a traditional Thanksgiving among only the immediate family. Breathing deeply, however, I agreed with Sage and we said our goodbyes.

"Have you come up with Plan C yet?" Mom asked.

"No. Let's keep pushing through. We're going to figure this out. Maybe we have Greg remove the plywood for that day, leaving the door wide open." Visions of the remaining glass littering the room again caused me to shutter. The plywood needs to stay in place until the window company can replace it. "I don't know, but we'll power through. Everything will work out fine."

We finished our sandwiches, and kept bantering about ideas for furniture placement, tables, and food stations or a buffet line. But my head throbbed thinking about it all, and now cleaning sounded preferable, so we each went back to our machines and fired them up again.

In the hallway, on my knees, I scrubbed at a stubborn stain on the carpet that I'd noticed earlier. Once that was dealt with, I proceeded into each of the bedrooms, vacuuming up bits and pieces from overturned furniture and drawers. Trying not to be consumed by the violation I still felt, I managed one step at a time, making my way through the rest of the house. Soon we both finished and lay spent on the sectional sofa.

"Will Greg be coming home each night or do they camp on the mountain?" Mom wanted to know.

"Tonight, unless they find Larry, I believe the plan is for the team to camp out. He took his backpack."

"I still can't believe he's missing."

"Me either."

From somewhere in the house, I heard my phone ringing. I grunted, getting up and then searched for the phone before the sound stopped. Finding it on my bed, I flopped down and answered. It was Bella.

"I hate to even ask, but are we still on for nine tomorrow morning? Or?"

"Yeah. I think we have everything scrubbed enough that we can function in here again." I really didn't have the energy to think beyond that, but for now, we'd see how the first cooking session went and take it from there. "Oh, it looks like JJ is calling. I'll see you in the morning!"

I switched over to talk to JJ. "What's up, my friend?"

"When you talked to Melissa previously, had she told

you much about their property manager?"

"No, not really. Only that they had one. Why?"

"What we've learned is interesting. Did you know he's a neighbor of yours?"

"Hmm. No, had no idea. What's his name?"

"Tiago Santos. His family originally came from Portugal. He married a Columbian. Her name is Kaya Arias. From what we've been able to gather, both families settled in the United States back in the forties. It sounds like the Santoses have rather large families. I believe I already mentioned that his wife has a housecleaning business, but I wonder if any of your neighbors had mentioned using her services?"

I explained to him, trying to remember the last time I'd talked to my neighbors. Living in an area where everyone worked outside of the home, we routinely drove straight into our garages when we returned home. Sadly, it was rare to actually visit much with the neighbors. Shadow and I conversed with a few of them on the coming or going from our runs, but only in the winter months, because in the summer we were outside far earlier than anyone else was awake.

"Where does Tiago live? On my block?"

"No, the next one over—close to your same street number, though. So, somewhere midway down the block."

"Hmm. No, I'm not recalling those names. Maybe if I saw a picture, he might look familiar. And, about my neighbors, it got me thinking that I should have already gone over to my closest ones and asked if they saw anything suspicious when someone—or several someones— unloaded my house contents." I glanced at my watch and saw it was getting close to suppertime. Maybe this was as good a time as any?

"I have a picture of Mr. Santos and his wife. I'll text you that now. If you recognize them, or any of your neighbors do, let me know."

"What exactly are you looking for?"

"I guess gossip, at this stage. I'm not sure. It seems strange to me they'd live in the Northeast Heights, given the type of jobs they have."

"JJ! Are you stereotyping?"

"No. C'mon, Libby. But you have to admit that it's a little pricey where you live. Modest, but not cheap. He does property maintenance and landscaping. She's a house cleaner. All respectable jobs, but nothing that can feed a family of eight *and* afford much more. I'm just saying."

"Whoa. *Eight kids?*"

"Well, six kids plus themselves. Sounds like they have other relatives they help provide for as well."

"Holy cow. Ambitious is what I'd call them."

"Yes, agreed. But I'd like to learn a little more … something seems off."

"Do you think he's involved with the murder?"

"I can't say that—but everyone involved with that property is a person of interest right now."

"What about the lady who died? Have you learned much more about her? What if she had a spouse or boyfriend who killed her?" I figured since JJ was being so open with me right now, I'd push my luck and ask as much as I could.

"She was married, but separated. Of course, her ex is also a person of interest. She lived across town in Glendale, so what she was doing at this house in Mesa, we haven't figured out yet. Her ex has an alibi, but we're still checking that out. He says he was with his new girlfriend—we're interviewing her tomorrow morning."

"So interesting. What did the deceased do for a living?"

"She was a lawyer."

"Hmm. For some reason, I wasn't expecting that."

"Now who is stereotyping?" He laughed. "Anyway, keep your ears open and if you learn anything, just let me know."

"Is Jeff Johnson actually asking for me to snoop around one of his cases?" I teased.

"Well, now, Libby … let's not get carried away. You said you needed to check in with the neighbors, anyway. Maybe in your conversation, someone can help us learn more about the Santos family."

"Sure, no problem, JJ."

We chatted about Greg's expedition and a few other family updates before he had to run off. After I hung up, I checked my watch again. Six o'clock. If I was going to find neighbors at home, I should get up and try now.

I struck out with the first door I knocked on, the one on the east side of me. So I crossed the street and as I strolled up the walkway, a gentleman opened the door and came outside.

"Hi, Libby," he greeted.

Not knowing whether he would remember me, I was pleased he had. "Hey, Craig. It's been a while."

"Yeah, been traveling a lot this year. You know how it goes."

I nodded. "Unfortunately, I don't have great news. Someone robbed my house in broad daylight. I'm curious whether you may have seen anything—or, maybe you have cameras that caught something?" I gave him the timing and details, as much as I knew.

"Oh, jeez! I'm sorry to hear that, Libby. Uh, no, wasn't home. I have cameras though and will look to see if there's anything to report. Did they make off with much?"

"Unfortunately. Not that I have a lot of valuables, but of course, there is a cost to replace everything. I think what makes me most mad is all the damage they've done inside. It's not like they casually pocketed a few items, but they literally tore my house apart. At least I'm assuming it was more than one person—with the extent of the damage and the amount of stuff that was hauled away."

We chatted awhile longer, and he promised to check his cameras. Before I walked away, I remembered to ask, "Do you use a cleaning service? You know, since you travel so often."

He shook his head. "It's just me here. I haven't needed to hire help."

We said our goodbyes, and I tried the house on either side of him before crossing the street again. Neither neighbor saw anything suspicious—one had exterior cameras and promised to look through her footage history. As I crossed to my side of the street again, I realized how disappointed I was that the police hadn't spoken to anyone yet. I would have thought that's where they'd start their investigation.

The neighbor to the west side of my house was home. Robin opened her door with a large smile on her face. "Libby, it's been so long! We really should get together more often. How's that sweet Labrador of yours?" Kids screeched in the background and one toddler ran up behind her, hiding behind her leg, and then peeking out at me. I gave her a little wave, and she tore off, joining her siblings in another room.

"Shadow? She's doing well."

"And I see you have quite a hunky man staying with you these days…"

I blushed. "Greg. Yes. We've been together a little more than a year now. Hey, I'm here to caution you actually…"

"What?"

"Yeah. Someone robbed my house yesterday—you didn't happen to be home between, say, ten and four?"

Her root-beer-colored eyes widened with terror. "No! You're kidding me? Libby—are you okay?"

"I wasn't home. But they did a number on my house and its contents. Mom and I have been cleaning up all day long."

"And just before the holidays … I can't believe it."

"Were you home during the day?"

"No, I took the kids to the zoo all day. We got home around dinnertime, I'd say."

"And this is the first time you're hearing about the crime?"

She nodded and her long, bottle-blonde hair tumbled down from its messy bun onto her shoulders. Sweeping strands away from her face, she gasped. "I'm shocked. Here? In *our* neighborhood?" Robin said, bending over to pick up the large decorative hair clip from the floor. She wrestled her hair back on top of her head and clipped it back in place.

"I know. I guess I thought the police would have reached out by now. Anyway, if you hear from other neighbors of any details—please let me know, or call the police. Keep your eyes open, though. And definitely keep your doors locked."

"Is that how they got into your house?"

"Actually, no. It isn't. They completely smashed my back sliding glass door, so I guess it didn't matter whether it was locked."

"Oh, dear Lord!" she exclaimed. "My children! We can't have things like this happen in *our* neighborhood. We're supposed to be safer here."

"I'm not sure what the motive was. It's not as though I have expensive belongings—why my house over anyone else's, I can't say. Just stay diligent, and oh, do you have cameras?"

"I've been telling Archie to get us some of those things! He's always so concerned about money—you know, with four little ones running around and all."

I hadn't remembered her husband's name, and couldn't recall that I'd ever actually met him before. Archie—I'd have to remember that. "I can't imagine so many kids. Do they have playmates in the neighborhood? I rarely see them outside playing."

"Oh, there are some families on the next blocks over— both directions—that we have playdates with sometimes."

"Do you know Tiago Santos, or his family, then?"

"Oh, of course! What a delightful family they are. Trying to find time to get together with Tiago and Kaya is a whole other thing. They are busy *all the time*. But I take in a couple of their youngest ones. How do you know them?"

I hadn't expected her to actually know them, so I just stated, "House cleaning."

"Oh, sure. She's great, isn't she?"

I slightly nodded in agreement. "How long has she

worked for you?"

"Oh, no. No, Archie would *never* pay for that service. That's my job since I stay home with the kids. I have some other friends who use her crew, though. They rave all the time about how they could never get their homes as clean, saying *it's worth it*. I wish … oh, how I wish." Her wistful gaze followed another squeal behind her. A crashing sound in the background snapped her back to attention. "Oh jeez, what are they into now? Listen, Libby, I'd just love to chat all evening—trust me. Adult talk over baby talk any day of the week! But I better get back to the littles, and Archie will expect his meal as soon as he gets home in…" she checked her watch and her eyes flew open. "Any minute! I gotta go!"

As I followed the sidewalk home, I mulled over what exactly to tell JJ about that encounter. I had found a neighbor who knew the Santos family, but had I truly learned anything important? What *had* JJ wanted me to learn about them, anyway? Hopefully, Robin had her hands so full she would forget I let on that I might know them. As seldom as I saw the neighbors, I wasn't too concerned about it. But it also wouldn't hurt to take a little walk and find out where these employees of the Barnsteads lived.

I set out at a brisk pace, walking past the houses I'd already visited, out of our cul-de-sac and to the main road into the development. I turned left, crossed the street, and turned left again. That's when I remembered JJ sent photos. I pulled the phone from my pocket, opening his text message and seeing the house number. It was three properties away and across the street.

I stood on the sidewalk, my gaze fixed on the house. It was a Spanish territorial style home, complete with a light tan stucco exterior, arched windows and doorways, wrought iron accents, red-tiled roof, and decorative tile-work. It had a beautiful courtyard patio, which featured beautifully trimmed hedging. Was this the same house I'd seen only days ago? The one I was near when that menacing figure Shadow chased vanished in the predawn light.

My right foot throbbed again as I recalled details of running barefoot after my dog. A vision of a tall and muscular man who had bright yellow shoes on, but no specific details I could make out other than that. His moves had been swift and deliberate, but had he really gone to *this* house? Had he actually been running from *us*? I remembered being so concerned about Shadow's limp that I'd lost sight of the man. How was it I suddenly felt as though he'd been a predator stalking his prey?

CHAPTER ELEVEN

Greg called around nine that night. They had made it several miles past the point where Larry's personal effects were found. Shadow hadn't found his scent yet, but they were hopeful of finding him near a well-known treasure hunter area. Greg mentioned that Larry had a long-standing fixation on the history of Spanish gold mining in the Superstition mountains.

"So, we'll head out again at dawn. There'll be another group, assisted by helicopter, who will search along the southern slopes of the mountain. And we've already put out the word, with printed flyers, for the many hikers along Siphon Draw. I still have doubts he went that direction, but since it's the popular hiking trail to Flat Iron, it makes sense to cover that area as well."

The connection kept breaking up and I hoped he could understand me. I think I got most of what he'd said. "Do you think foul play could be involved?"

"I really don't know what to think. I'm still going along the lines that he may have twisted an ankle or something. Anyway, what else is going on? You holding it together?"

I filled him in on the conversations I'd had with JJ and the little bit I'd learned about the property manager who lived in our neighborhood. There wasn't much to tell, but I still found it disconcerting about the man Shadow ran after, and then finding that the Santos family home was right there. Coincidence? Normally I didn't buy into things happening by chance.

"Are you still cooking tomorrow? I mean, no one is going to blame you if you'd rather call this whole thing off."

I sighed, understanding the truth behind his statement. "Yeah, I know. But we're still on for the first round of cooking in the morning. How are your parents? Dana and the kids? Am I being insensitive by doing this? More importantly, should I be there with them?"

"No, there's nothing for you to do at this end yet, but I have told them to call you should they need anything. Yeah, I think they're worried about Larry, but after all these years, I also believe the family knows not to be *too concerned.*" He cleared his throat and collected his thoughts. "We'll find him. Then it will be nice for everyone to gather with your fantastic meal at the end of the week. I gotta say—I love how persistent you are in this endeavor."

Relaxed, stretched out on my bed, I could see his classic smile in my mind—the one that shines through his eyes. I missed him and prayed he and Shadow would return tomorrow with Larry.

$* * *$

The next day, the first cooking session commenced. My friends, Cody and Brad, Sage, and Bella, all brought their family recipes. Lexi, my mother, and I were there to be their sous chefs and taste testers.

Brad took the lead, mixing all the ingredients, and telling us the history of *lefse*. In his family's Norwegian lineage, the potato-based flatbread was traditionally a Christmas holiday treat.

"Since Norwegians have immigrated to America, it's now common for families to make this at Thanksgiving, too. Simple ingredients: the potatoes are the star of the show and then we'll cream together the butter, salt, sugar, and fold in flour until well blended. From this dough, we'll make them into flat rounds."

"Sounds exactly like tortillas from our region," Bella noted.

Cody nodded, tilting his head. "You could say that— they look identical. The potatoes give them a unique taste, though."

Brad turned off the mixer and demonstrated what he wanted us to do. "Grab a handful of the dough and work it into a ball, like this. Then, at your station, roll it out into a round flatbread. The key is to roll them really thin, without tearing them. My handy husband here has already cut pieces of parchment paper; please stack one lefse each between a piece of paper once it's flattened. We'll ultimately stack a whole bunch of them and store them in these containers. Let's work on making all the balls first, then we'll divide them up amongst us."

As we went to work, Cody shared with us some fun

facts about Norwegian holidays.

My mom cut in. "Cody, are you also Norwegian?"

He nodded. "My mom's side of the family has distant relatives born in Norway. All of my immediate family were born in the United States, though. Grandma thought it was important to keep some traditions alive, but I'd say my mother let many of them slip away over the years."

He told us all about *Julenissen*, who was a fairy tale creature widely thought to have delivered gifts on Christmas Eve—very similar to Santa Claus. Apparently, he also wore red, had a beard, but people knew him as the *Norse nisse*, a playful mythological creation associated with the winter solstice. Also similar to how we leave cookies for Santa, Norwegians would leave a bowl of rice porridge with butter for Julenissen.

"So, they didn't leave lefse for him?" Bella questioned.

Cody laughed. "Nope, but I suppose they could have!"

I was curious. "What other common holiday foods the Norwegians eat?"

Brad was happy to answer. "Typically, lots of fish. Pork belly for some families. Sausages and meatballs are popular. And, of course, gravy on everything."

Bella's nose scrunched up. "I'm happy we have turkey and stuffing."

We continued to roll out small thin flatbreads, stacking them at each of our stations until we'd finished with all the dough.

"We have enough to feed an army, Brad," I noted as we piled the parchment paper stacks into a large casserole dish to refrigerate.

"I know. This recipe makes *so* many. I will fry them up in a skillet Thanksgiving morning before we come over.

What we don't eat, we'll give away to each family as lefse leftover gifts." Brad's smile lit up the room. "Here, let's cook up some now for each of us—it can be our breakfast right now! Libby, we'll need some butter. And do you have cinnamon and sugar?"

I nodded and went to the pantry to retrieve them, checking my phone for messages as I did. I couldn't get past the feeling that I should do more for the Lawsons than I was.

As Cody and Brad carefully cooked, I got a pot of coffee brewing. Before long, the aroma of butter, cinnamon, and sugar filled the kitchen and we sat around the breakfast bar enjoying the Norwegian delicacy.

Brad swallowed his bite, rolling his eyes in ecstasy. "So good. Now, I'm uncertain if the cinnamon and sugar addition would be considered *traditional*, but it is how my mom always served lefse, so I've continued her tradition."

My mom agreed. "It's perfect. Very good, Brad."

There were moans of agreement all around as we stuffed our faces.

"Who's next to cook after our lefse breakfast break?" Lexi asked.

"I'll go—mine are super easy," Bella volunteered. "Sorry, there weren't many holiday traditions in my family, but we were very good at making pigs in a blanket and I learned those are English. And, apparently, my birth father's family was from Great Britain!"

Bella and I cleared the kitchen counters while the others finished their coffee. She pulled out the canned, refrigerated dough and the packages of miniature, cheese-filled beef sausages.

"Compared to others, mine is almost embarrassingly

easy," she said, chuckling.

"We can never have enough finger foods to keep everyone occupied, especially with all the kids. Besides, with Greg's family around for yet another week, we'll be so grateful for all the leftovers." I chuckled, then glanced down at my phone when it chimed.

I was hoping for Greg to bring news that they had already found Larry, but my hopes were dashed. My heart did a little jump when I saw it was JJ, though. Before I answered, my eyes cast over to the table where Lexi was chatting with the group. I punched the button on the phone and quietly walked out of the room and down the hallway.

"Hi, JJ."

"Hey there! Just curious how it went, talking to your neighbors?"

I filled him in, letting him know I hadn't really learned much, but everyone assured me they'd look at their camera footage.

"Well, I think I might have something for you then. We have a neighbor who reported footage of a white van leaving your cul-de-sac around two-thirty the day of the break-in. It's a little grainy, but we're trying to get plate numbers now. That's not the only interesting news, though. We think this could be the same van found in footage leaving the Barnstead's rental property during the early morning hours on the suspected day of the murder!"

"Oh, wow. Are the two cases related, do you think? It can't be a coincidence, can it?"

"Can't say for sure. What I do know is that we're bringing Kaya back in for more questioning. My bets are on those plates being registered to her cleaning company."

"I could see that, at least for the Barnstead's property. But why would they be at *my* house? What could the connection possibly be?"

"Maybe there isn't a connection. I'm not sure. And, hey, let's keep this between us for now."

"Of course. Which neighbor had the footage? I'm a little surprised no one told me."

He gave me the address, and I realized it was one I hadn't found anyone at home yesterday. "It would be great if my other neighbors closest to me had footage that supported this and also showed more detail."

"True. I may have some time later this afternoon to stop by and pay them a visit."

After hanging up, I walked back into the kitchen to find everyone rolling up sausages into little dough blankets. One cookie sheet full of the pastries was ready, so I checked with Bella on the timing and popped them into the oven. It didn't take long until we'd completed four dozen pigs in a blanket and had them on cooling racks.

Cody turned to Sage Logan with a slight scowl on his face. "Please don't tell me you're making Haggis?"

Her hearty laughter filled the room. "No, I wouldn't subject this crowd to our most famous Scottish holiday fare."

"What is Haggis?" Bella wondered.

"A pudding made with a sheep's insides, basically," Brad added.

"Ewww," several of us exclaimed.

Still laughing, Sage shushed everyone. "You really have to try it before you knock it. And remember, *pudding* is not the same as we know in America. Haggis is a savory pie, and you'd probably never even know you were eating a sheep's internal organs."

Another round of protests and she gave up trying to convince the Americans that haggis was delicious.

"So, what are you going to make instead?"

"Well, since Logan was my first husband's name, you all have it wrong, and why I won't be making anything Scottish. I'm actually staying very traditional and sticking with an American Thanksgiving side dish." As she continued her explanation, she pulled out bags from the refrigerator. "We're going to prepare the stuffing ahead of time. This gives it the opportunity to really seal in the flavors. On Thursday, I'll bake it before I bring it over."

"Won't that make it super mushy? Might as well stuff the turkey, then." It was common knowledge that Lexi disliked soggy bread.

Smiling broadly, Sage assured the crowd. "Oh, no. Trust me. This is a great recipe and I promise, no soggy bread."

Everyone watched intently as she pulled out fresh sage, onions, celery, garlic, chicken broth, two rolls of breakfast sausage, eggs, bread crumbs, and dried cranberries.

"Libby, we'll need butter and a fairly large stock pot. CB, you're in charge of dicing celery and onion. Lexi, can you please pull the sage from the stems and rough chop? I'll get started browning the sausage."

I couldn't help smile when Sage used Greg's nickname, CB, for Cody and Brad. It seemed everyone had embraced the nomenclature for the handsome couple now. They both hopped right into action, peeling the onion, washing the produce, and each chopping on separate cutting boards.

Bella grabbed the stock pot, handed it to Sage, and watched as she drizzled some olive oil inside it. She accepted the onion and celery from the guys and watched them sizzle for a few seconds before adding the sausage.

"Oh wow, that already smells delicious." My mom had made herself busy mincing the garlic cloves. She added them to the pot when instructed to, along with the fresh sage. Then she went about spraying several large baking dishes and setting them along the countertop nearest the stove.

"Okay, I'm ready for the chicken broth now."

I poured from a large measuring cup into the stockpot.

"We'll let this come to boiling and then add the bread, cranberries, and egg." Sage walked over to another bag she had sitting on the far end of the counter. "I seasoned, cubed, and dried ciabatta bread yesterday." She pulled out several large bags, and we each snuck a piece before it went into the boiling stock.

Brad was in heaven. "I'd be happy with just this." He snuck an extra piece of bread and popped it into his mouth.

Once the pot was at a full boil, Sage stirred the mixture until there was no more liquid. She turned off the burner while saying, "And that's it—so easy!" She stirred in the eggs and mixed thoroughly, then divided the stuffing between the various baking dishes. "I'll take these home and refrigerate, then bake them until crispy on top before I come over on Thursday."

"I've never added all these extras into stuffing, but it smells absolutely delightful. Can't wait to try it!" I got scolded when I approached with a spoon.

"Not yet, Libby. Still have to bake—we have raw eggs in there."

Lexi's nose scrunched in disgust.

By the time Sage set the stockpot into the kitchen

sink, Bella already had all the other dishes washed. I was shocked to see that it was already mid-afternoon—where had the time gone?

Brad and Cody announced they needed to get to the theater for a function. Lexi needed to pick up Joshua from the sitter. Everyone packed up their items to take home, and for those who were helping the next day, we agreed on the same time, same place. We'd bake pies, mash the potatoes, and Lexi planned on an extra special green bean casserole.

That would leave us only the turkey to roast on Thanksgiving Day, which turned out to be the best decision I could've made, when everything else fell apart.

CHAPTER TWELVE

The doorbell rang, and before I could get out of my chair, my phone pinged. I glanced at the phone, stopping in my tracks. It was Greg. More banging at the door jolted me into forward motion again and I also pushed the button, answering the call.

"Are you okay?" I asked Greg, quietly peeking through my door's peephole. There was a blonde-haired woman standing with her back to me. Then I saw a little guy toddling away and Robin chasing him.

"Yeah, why? Er, why ask that way?"

"The doorbell just rang—can I call you back? Think it's the neighbor."

"Oh, sure. Just wanted to let you know we found Larry."

The doorbell rang again.

"Oh good! I'll call you right back."

"I might be out of range for a while—then with the police. But, should be home by tonight. Just wanted to let you know that."

I opened the door, and a little one whooshed right by my leg. "Okay, see you tonight." And I hung up.

"I'm sorry, Libby," Robin pushed by me, chasing after her son. "He is fast." She picked him up and struggled to hold on to him as he thrashed to get back down.

"Well, hello, Robin. What's up?"

"If I can get Arlo to stop moving for half a second…" he screamed out, bit her arm, and she lowered him to the ground. "Owww! You little sh…" He ran off down the hall. She started off after him. "Get back here, Arlo. Now!"

"I don't think there's anything he could…" I called after them, then heard a crash, and followed them into the guest room my mom was staying in.

He was up on the dresser top and knocked off everything mom had set out: perfume, her journal, a teacup, and a vase of flowers. Luckily, the glassware didn't break when it hit the padded carpeting.

"Arlo!" she swept him up in her arms again, giving him a swat on his diapered bottom. "Stop that. This is not your house."

I had to wonder whether he behaved this way in their own home, although I figured theirs was probably fully baby-proofed, whereas mine was definitely not.

She tried hanging on tight to the constant squirmer. "I wanted to let you know Archie wasn't surprised when I told him about your break-in. He has seen someone lurking around—about a week ago when he was last home."

"Does he have a description? Has he called the police?"

"No, he's away on a business trip again—seems he's always traveling these days. But he said he hadn't worried about it since you lock your side gate just the same way we do. We're safe." As she said the last words, her expression changed. "Ohhh, *was* your gate locked?"

"Funny you ask … the day before the break-in, Shadow woke me up. She heard something outside." I recounted the story to her, explaining how I found the gate opened and how Shadow got out. "So, double check yours too. Just in case."

She looked panicked. "I haven't checked. I better do that."

"What else did Archie say … male, female? Whose house were they nearest—yours? Mine?"

She struggled again with her child. "You know, he made it sound like no big deal. I mean, he hadn't recognized who it was, but I honestly don't know how he would recognize *anyone*. He's gone so much. Anyway, that's good information about the lock—I'll go check. I've got to get these kids fed, too." Her arms gripped Arlo tighter as she hissed, "Would you *stop it*!"

I watched them leave through the front door, amazed at how much stamina that woman had. *Were all kids this high maintenance?*

Mom drove up before I stepped back inside. I helped her unload groceries.

"I still need to find fresh cranberries—they were all out," she said as she set the bags she carried on the kitchen counter. "And the restoration company called—I need to go meet them over at the house."

"I have great news—they found Larry!"

She set her purse down on the barstool. "Oh, that's

fantastic. Is he okay?"

I realized then I didn't know the answer to the question. Although Greg hadn't mentioned going to the hospital, but surely, they'd have to.

"I've gotta call Greg back. Then we'll go by your house and to that farmer's market. I'm sure they'll have the cranberries. Wait, the restoration people are coming today? I thought the work would not start at your house until next week, after the holiday?"

"Yeah, I'm not sure what they're going to do, but I've got to get over there to let them in the house."

We got the groceries put away, and then I tried calling Greg back. The phone rang several times and went to voice mail. I hung up and dialed Dana's phone instead.

"Have they found him?" she asked immediately upon answering.

"Oh, you haven't heard?" I thought Greg would've called his family first.

"Heard what?"

"Yes, they found him! I know little more than that, but Greg called me and said they were on their way down the mountain. It wasn't a great connection."

"I've gotta call the parents then. Are you coming out here?"

I hadn't planned on it until that moment, but she'd sounded desperate. "Of course. I'm on my way." As soon as I hung up, I turned to my mother. "I need to get over to Dana's. Are you okay meeting the repair guys on your own?"

She nodded, and we each headed our own directions.

As I drove up Quail Lane, I waved at Sage, who was out watering some plants at her house next door to Greg's property. Farther up the road where it dead-ended, I saw that Anne and Bill had already arrived. I didn't spot Greg's vehicle, which made sense. I was sure Larry would need a medical check, at the very least. Hopefully not hospitalization, though. My heart thumped, wondering what had happened to him, but I decided not to pester by calling again. It would be soon enough that we'd hear the entire story.

Dana met me at my car door before I could even turn the engine off.

"Mom and Dad are getting antsy. Do you have any updates?"

I shook my head. "It'll take some time to get off the mountain, I suppose. I know Greg will contact one of us as soon as he has cell coverage again."

As we walked up to his fifth-wheel, I took in the scenery of the majestic Superstition Mountains. Ever since Greg bought this land, I'd been admiring the views. He talks as though one day we'll build our dream home here. At first, I thought that was quite presumptive on his part—considering I lived within walking distance of my business. However, as I continued to admire the dramatic mountain range and the lush Sonoran desert landscape, I was gradually changing my mind. Afterall, it's only about ten miles from work, even though it feels so remote.

I realized I'd tuned out most of Dana's chatter. "Wait. What was that last part?"

"Mom is talking about leaving. Going home tomorrow!"

"What?" My heart sank. I knew I should have spent more time with them and less worrying about the meal planning.

"I know. But maybe you can help me talk her into

staying." She opened the door and we found Anne and Bill sitting on the sofa, each with a soda in hand. They stood, set down their drinks, and reached out to give me a hug.

"Are you guys doing okay?" I asked.

Bill hemmed and hawed. "It's been a lot, Libby. Have you heard anything more about our son?"

"Not yet. But we'll know more soon."

"Look, Libby…" Anne began.

"Mom, let's just get Larry back here and then decide, alright?"

She scowled at her daughter. "Dana, let me talk now." Anne turned to me and offered a grim smile and spoke in a soft voice. "Libby, there's been so much—of course, the murder, the fire at your mother's, the break-in at your home, and now this with Larry. Forgive us if we might just be a little overwhelmed and thinking we should head home."

"Oh, Anne. Now that we've found Larry, I really hope you'll change your mind. Everything will be fine." With as genuine a smile as I could muster, I added, "Plus, we have a ton of food already prepared and much more to go. We'll all get into the spirit, you'll see." *Would we? How much was this me trying to convince myself instead of her?*

Anne's expression did not exude hope, but I continued with the positive talk, filling them in on the cooking we did today. I assured her she'd have a blast with the group tomorrow when we baked pies and all. Ultimately, I received a wider smile and her eyes showed a brief glimmer of hope.

Dana chimed in. "Hey, let's dump the soda and open a bottle of wine to celebrate!"

I glanced at my watch. It certainly could be time for

happy hour. Now, I only prayed Larry and Greg would walk through the door any moment.

CHAPTER THIRTEEN

"Mom, what do you mean, 'someone destroyed all the walls in your house'?"

"Just that. They punched giant holes in the kitchen and living room walls and tore down the sheet rock. Then, once they looked within the walls, they confirmed there's been fire and water damage throughout. They will have to replace all the walls, the flooring, and all the cabinetry."

I couldn't remember whether they'd mentioned that as a possibility the first time we met with them, but it sure agitated my mother now.

"I had to give them the down payment—fifty-thousand dollars!"

"What? I thought it would all go through insurance."

"Hopefully, they'll reimburse. The guy said in order to

begin the work, they'd need the money today."

Something sounded fishy, but I was hesitant to get her worked up more than she already was. "Look, Mom, we'll call the insurance company in the morning and get it sorted. Did you write a check—or how…?"

"No, they said cash only. So, I went to the bank and withdrew the money."

"What? Are you kidding me? Are they still there?"

Surprised she had that much in her account readily available, my heart sank. None of this was as the company described to us only days ago. *What changed?*

"No, they just drove off. This house is such a disaster—I thought we'd have time to remove some belongings first."

"So did I. Well, lock up and we'll meet you over at my house soon."

"Hold on. How's Larry?"

"We're still waiting to hear."

"Oh, no. I hope he's alright."

"Me too. See you soon, Mom."

The evening air had turned cool, while we sat watching the sunset colors change on the mountain. After I'd hung up, Dana saw the concern on my face and I explained to the group what my mom related about the home repairs. Bill's eyebrows lifted and then one eye squinted.

"All that should go through the insurance company. She shouldn't have to pay cash up front. That just doesn't sound right."

I agreed with him, voicing my own concerns. My phone rang, and I indicated to the group it was Greg, before I stood and put him on speakerphone.

"Libby, take me off speaker, please," he requested, and I did so immediately.

"Oh. What's going on?" I turned my back on the group, taking a few steps away from them.

"Listen, I don't want to worry Mom, but Larry is being transported to the hospital in an ambulance."

"Oh, okay," I answered, trying to keep calm. I turned slightly back to the group, seeing that all eyes were on me. "And where is that?"

"Desert Samaritan."

"Would you like us to meet you there?"

"I'll come home and we can all go together."

"Okay, I'm out at your trailer with the family."

"Good. Even closer. See you in about fifteen minutes."

As we walked into the emergency room, a flood of memories came rushing back. Those from when I was a teenager and my father died. And then those from more recent events—I *hate* hospitals. The smells, the emotions, the bad news.

Anne and Bill held each other close, and we guided them to a seat in the waiting room. Dana and her kids sat quietly on either side of them. Greg went to the desk to ask questions. I vaguely overheard 'he's in surgery,' but nothing else.

Greg simply stated to his parents, "We should know something soon. Can I get you guys some water, coffee, anything?"

I walked down the hallway with Greg and we found the vending machines where we got a couple sodas, waters, and some snacks.

"What happened?" I asked Greg. "Surgery for what?"

"Oh, you overheard that?"

I nodded. "Is he going to be okay?"

"He'll be fine. His foot is a mess, though. I'm not sure of the extent, but he definitely couldn't walk. The EMTs brought him down the mountain on a litter."

"A *litter*?"

"Yeah, a lightweight stretcher, essentially."

"He was conscious, right?"

"Yep. In a ton of pain!"

"Did he tell you what happened? Where did you find him? And what about his phone and belongings that were found?"

"I'm going to have to tell the whole family—let's take these to them," he said, holding up the water bottles. "I'd rather not repeat the story."

"And Shadow did good?" I asked as we walked back to the waiting room.

"She was amazing! She found him—couldn't have done it without her." He planted a kiss on top of my head. "I'm sure she's sleeping back at the trailer. Full tummy now—yep, she'll be tired. That was quite the hike."

Bill stood as we approached. "Son, we have to know what's going on. This is killing your mother."

"I know. I know. Take a seat, Dad." He handed everyone their drinks and some snacks to pass around. Then he launched into the rescue story. "First off, Larry is going to be just fine. He encountered some unsavory fellows on the trail apparently. He's a little beat up and got lost. Thankfully, Shadow led us right to him so he wasn't out there any longer than he was."

Bill stopped his son. "Who beat him up?"

"We don't know."

"Thank goodness he's alright," Anne muttered.

Greg shook his head.

Dana and I held each other's hand, listening to details about the rescue and carrying Larry down the mountain. Anne held her face in her hands and didn't want to hear anymore.

Finally, the doctor came through the door into the waiting room. "Lawson," he called out.

Greg and Bill stood, and the doctor approached. "Family of Larry Lawson?" They nodded, and then he told us that Larry would be fine. "He broke his foot," he explained, giving us all the details about how many tiny bones there are in the foot and how fragile they are. He had to place a couple of pins to hold things together. "It will help him heal faster and gain strength in his ankle again. Anyway, once he comes out of the anesthesia, he can have a couple of visitors. I suggest the rest of you go home for the night. Most likely, he'll get released tomorrow." He gave us a tired smile and asked if we had questions.

Everyone thanked the doctor and let out a collective sigh of relief. Anne and Bill stayed behind with Larry while we took Dana and the kids back to the trailer.

CHAPTER FOURTEEN

Shadow was a bundle of energy early the next morning. I hooked her leash on, leaving Greg and my mom to enjoy their coffee. We started out at a jog, but ended up running for over five miles at a good clip. At the turnoff to my neighborhood, Shadow abruptly stopped, and I nearly stumbled over her.

"What's wrong, girl?" I looked in the direction her nose pointed, but nothing stood out to me. "C'mon, I'd like some coffee, and still need to shower before the gang arrives for more cooking." I tugged a couple times and ultimately, she gave in and we proceeded a few feet before I saw the large black SUV come around the corner.

It slowed as it passed by us. Shadow barked ferociously, lunging at the vehicle. Gripping tightly at her leash, I commanded, "Shadow, no!" Thinking they were going to pull over and stop, I backed up and pulled her toward me. "C'mon, let's go the other way," I urged my dog, as I looked into the darkened windows to see who it was. All I could see was my reflection.

I had Shadow's attention now, and we ran off in the other direction, taking another route home. Despite constantly wanting to, I focused all my attention forward and never looked back to see if we were followed.

Huffing and puffing as I removed Shadow's leash safely in the hallway, I quickly made my way inside the kitchen, where my mother and Greg still sat chatting. The mischievous look on my mom's face as I entered had me do a double-take.

"What? What happened?" I breathlessly asked.

They made brief eye contact and shrugged, both saying *nothing* in unison.

I filled a reusable K-cup with my favorite blend of coffee and popped it into the machine. While that brewed, I pulled out some flavored creamer from the fridge. It was only something I treated myself to now and then; normally, I'd take my coffee black.

"When are the troops arriving?" Greg asked, taking a bite of his toast.

"Around nine. I'm guessing your mom won't be joining?"

"I doubt it. They'll be eager to pick up Larry when he's released."

"Have you heard anything yet on his release?"

He shook his head as he swallowed and took another sip of coffee.

"What about those guys that beat him up? Any news on catching them?"

He shook his head again. "That's the wildest story, isn't it?"

I poured in the creamer and joined them sitting at the breakfast bar. "We've hiked those hills so many times. I couldn't imagine running into thugs like that. There has to be more to that story; I can't wait to hear it from Larry himself."

"I know. Something doesn't add up, and I'm praying he truly didn't know the guys or hadn't somehow instigated the attack."

Mom was curious. "How would he know them?"

"Yeah, I don't know what to think. Based on my parents' reactions, there is definitely something they aren't saying."

My stomach rumbled. "That toast smells good. Want another piece? I'm going to toast some." I stood and opened the bag, pulling out several slices, when both of them nodded their heads.

"Mom, we need to call the insurance company this morning."

"Why?"

"Because we need to be sure they're sending a reimbursement check for that fat deposit you paid in cash yesterday."

Greg's head whipped around toward Julia. "What cash payment? Related to the fire repairs?"

One of Mom's legs fidgeted, and her cheeks burned with shame. Without looking at him directly, she simply said, "Uh, yeah. Libby's already chastised me, so please. It'll be fine."

Looking skeptically in Greg's direction, I carefully pulled the toasted bread out and plopped it on a plate. I grabbed one piece and spread peanut butter over it. Next, I put on a thin layer of apricot preserves, and then took a bite, savoring the sweet and salty flavors.

"I just don't understand why they made such a mess yesterday—I thought we had more time to get my stuff out first."

My eyebrows lifted, again trying not to be judgmental, but also trying to relate silently to my boyfriend how I thought the whole thing was very suspicious.

He suggested to Julia, "Let's go over there. I want to see what they did. And, yes, Libby is correct. We need to inform the insurance company about that payment immediately. It probably would have been best to get them on the phone yesterday when the crew asked for payment."

She hung her head. "I know. I know. Let me get cleaned up and dressed and we can go over." She slunk out of the room and down the hallway.

Greg turned to me. "What do you suspect?"

"That she's been had. I asked her more last night and she couldn't tell me the name of the company that showed up. She said there were two pickup trucks; you know, work trucks with ladder racks and toolboxes on them. But she wasn't sure the name and logo of the company were on either of them. Something doesn't sit right with me on this because when we first met with the restoration people the other day, they never mentioned an upfront deposit. Now, they demand thousands?"

"I see what you're saying, but maybe it's all on the up and up."

"All in *cash?* I think it's because she showed up alone. Had either of us been there, would they have done the same thing?"

He shrugged and finished his coffee. "Well, let's see what the insurance company has to say."

"Do you think you can help her with that? I've got all the…"

"Absolutely. No problem, hon. And then I'm going to catch up with the family and see about Larry. Hopefully, they'll be back at the trailer by then. Oh! Any further word from JJ and what's going on in the murder investigation?"

"I haven't heard any more about that. I'm hoping I'll have time today to get with him though. He's supposed to be interviewing some of our neighbors."

"Really?"

"I guess there's camera footage that possibly shows the same van in the neighborhood as was in the Barnsteads' rental's neighborhood."

"Interesting." Greg stood, kissed me on the forehead, and then cleaned his mug out in the sink before heading off to shower.

* * *

The morning passed by like a whirlwind. Lexi, Dana and her kids, Jordan and her kids, Bella, CB, and I stayed plenty busy baking pies. Lexi showed us a few spicy tricks with her pumpkin pie recipe and she whipped up a couple of pecan pies that turned out perfectly. Dana, Jordan, and all the kids peeled and chopped apples, pecans, and ginger. Bella, Cody, and Brad assisted as sous chefs today. My nieces, Apple and Annie, and I put together my mother's delicious apple cranberry pie.

Apple stirred the fresh cranberries into the apple pie mixture, and I watched as my mom guided her granddaughters through the process.

"I want to own a bakery someday!" Annie stated.

Apple smiled widely. "We should open Apple Annie's Pie Shoppe! We'll make such unique flavor combinations—people will come from all over the state to get our pies."

Cody and Brad cheered on the young entrepreneurial spirit, and we all chimed in with ideas.

"How fun would that be?" I asked. "I feel like I've heard that name somewhere before, though."

"Down in Wilcox—if it's not Apple Annie's, it's something close to it." Bella picked up the mixing bowls and carried them to the sink, when she noticed how deflated both Apple and Annie became. "Hey! Don't worry—by the time you open your pie shop, it will be completely unique. Don't give up on your dreams."

Their eyes perked up again, and they helped their grandmother tent the pie before putting it in the oven. After baking all the confections, we stirred together the ingredients for the green bean casserole and mashed both golden and sweet potatoes. Then we stored everything away in the refrigerator and collapsed in the living room.

"Whew! It feels like we're literally feeding an army," I said.

"How many are planning on coming now? I heard JJ mention our party to one of the officers who said he had no family here." Hesitantly, Lexi added, "I hope that was okay?"

"Oh yeah, he ran it by me first. I mean, what's one more person? I think we have close to thirty who have confirmed they'll be here."

Lexi's eyes widened in shock. "I've never hosted, or been to, a Thanksgiving meal of that size. Where are you going to fit everyone?"

I looked around the room again, seeing the plywood

still in place on my back slider and remembering that was a large part of the original plan. "We'll work it out—everything is figureoutable." I smiled, trying to reassure everyone that I wasn't panicking internally. My stomach churned, though; I really didn't have a clue what I was doing, much less agreeing with others when they wanted to add to the guest list. That was me, though; the more the merrier, I've always said.

About an hour later, I walked the last of my friends to the door. "Okay, don't forget—we're beginning with lefse and mimosas at nine on Thursday morning. Parades, munchies, and lots of camaraderie—don't be late! It'll be a fun-filled day." I closed the door behind them and took a deep breath. *Everything would work out perfectly.*

With the morning behind me, I would check in at the spa and then get in touch with JJ. As soon as I walked through the spa front door, I knew I shouldn't have added one more thing to my list today.

CHAPTER FIFTEEN

Kathleen, one of our top therapists, greeted me with that kind of grin which should have signaled for me to run.

"I'm so glad you stopped by!" she chimed. "Mrs. Barnstead is in the Serenity Room and has been after me to call you in." Kathleen kneeled down and got a face full of Shadow. "You are such a sweet girl! I've missed you around here!"

"Why?"

She stood back up, wiping hair off her clothing. "She wants one of *your* massages."

"I have this week off," I checked my watch, as though that proved how busy I was. Plus, JJ's voice entered my consciousness. I was supposed to keep my distance from the Barnsteads for right now.

"I know. And that's why I haven't called you."

Both of our heads turned, and my stomach lurched as the glass doors opened between the relaxation room and the lobby. Shadow woofed in surprise and then ran over to her.

"I thought I heard your voice!" Melissa Barnstead exclaimed, holding her hand out and telling Shadow, no. "Ugh, dogs."

"Shadow, come here," I called. She obediently sat at my side and I looped one finger

under her halter to ensure she'd stay with me.

"I'm *sooo* glad you're here," Melissa said to me, before turning to Kathleen. "Thank you for calling her. I was certain once she knew *I* was here, she'd come right away."

"How can I help you, Melissa? I'm sure Kathleen told you this week is my vacation; we

have family in town, as you know."

"Yes. Well, this is more important. Can we talk?" She tilted her head inside the Serenity

Room. "In private?"

Seemed fairly rude. I sighed, giving a nod to Kathleen. "I'll be right back. Can you watch Shadow for a minute?"

She agreed and pulled a treat from Cody's front desk drawer. Shadow sat at attention while I snuck by and rounded the front counter, passing through the door Kathleen held open. She walked straight through to the next set of doors—the ones which led to the massage therapy rooms and the office. I followed her.

"You are going to want to hear the latest debacle my husband's in now. And, you might as

well work on me while we're talking..." she announced.

"Melissa…"

"Oh, c'mon. Please…" she pouted, then continued walking to one of the therapy rooms

with an open door.

I wanted an update. I guess it couldn't hurt to spend a little more time here than I'd planned; JJ doesn't have to know.

"Alright. But only thirty minutes—I really have places I need to be." I quickly checked my spa phone app to be sure the room was available for the next hour. It was. I pulled out clean sheets and dressed the table before turning back to her. "Okay, you know the drill. I'll give you some privacy and I'll be back in a few minutes."

"I'll pay you handsomely."

I walked out and set my purse down in the office. Shadow stretched out on her bed when I came into the room. "You're such a good girl. I'll be back soon." I scratched the top of her head and gave her another treat; she remained on her bed.

Knocking on the therapy room door, I asked, "Are you ready, Melissa?"

"Ready!"

Slowly, I opened the door and confirmed she was under the sheet on the table. "Okay, so give me the details." I pulled off my shoes and hopped up on the sink, where I sanitized my feet. All part of the protocol for Ashiatsu, or barefoot, massage.

"Oh, Libby, it's horrible! The whole thing is just horrific."

"A woman was found dead, of course, it is." I dried off my feet, stepped down from the sink's countertop, and grabbed the massage oil.

She let out a strong huff. "No, no, not that. Fred has been *cheating on me.*" A muffled sniffle sounded. "And what's worse ... I don't think this skank was the first!"

I rubbed oil over Melissa's back and stepped up onto the massage table, reaching for the bars above me.

"Are you certain? He admitted to it?" I'd known this couple for a few years and never suspected there was anything but love between them.

"Well, no, he hasn't admitted to it. But I'm certain he is."

"Do you have any idea *who* he's stepping out with?" Then it dawned on me. "Please don't tell me she was the woman found in your rental..."

She hesitated, then muttered, "No, no ... I don't think so."

"Does his cheating have anything to do..."

"I really doubt it."

"And you don't have suspicions about anyone specific?"

"Oh, I don't know for sure. I've had my eyes on our property manager's wife, though. She's a bombshell. At least for a housekeeper."

"What?"

"I've suspected it for some time. Late nights and always some work-related excuse to leave what we're doing together. I mean, who could blame him, with her sultry ways and all? She is drop-dead gorgeous." She let out a sigh. "It's part of the reason I was insistent that we spend more time at our property in Mexico. To get him away from our rental properties here in the valley."

I wasn't sure what to say. Honestly, I was uncomfortable learning such private matters and couldn't imagine why she felt compelled to tell me such things. I kept working my heels into her upper back muscles, listening to my client, and trying not to be too judgmental.

"Then I learned she was down in Puerto Peñasco! I should have known—he started his late-night work excuses not long after we got there as well."

"Do you guys sell real estate in Mexico?"

"Oh yeah. Can't get away from it."

"Oh. I guess I was under the impression that was only your getaway."

"It was supposed to be," she cried. I could feel her back rise and fall with ragged breath as emotions consumed her.

"I'm sorry, Melissa."

"The worst part for me now is that we are this close to Thanksgiving and have *no plans*. Our friends are all in Mexico—that's where we were supposed to be for the holiday. And now, with everything, we're stuck here and I certainly don't feel like cooking." Another sniffle, and I offered her a tissue.

I eased myself off the table, grabbed the box of Kleenex, and handed her one. By the time I climbed back onto the table, I actually felt sorry for her.

"You could join our Thanksgiving celebration, if you'd like."

"Really? That would be okay?"

"Sure. The more, the merrier!" I grimaced, saying it out loud, but thankfully her head was still face down in the cradle.

"You're such a sweetheart. I'd be honored." Her voice cracked and tears began flowing again.

From that point, we both kept quiet. I used my feet to dig in further, working out her tight muscles. Other than a few more sniffles, she'd apparently got out what she wanted to say. There was something about her tabletop confession that hadn't settled well for me, though. Earlier, I swore she said she'd like to give me an update on their case. *Hadn't she said that?* Didn't that imply a connection between the extramarital problems and the death of the woman at that rental? *I'd really like to know more about the woman they found dead at that house.*

Thirty minutes was up in no time, and I left the room so Melissa could get dressed. Shortly afterward, I found her in the Serenity Room again with a hot cup of tea. Her eyes looked red and swollen and I felt for the lady. Sitting down next to her, I patted her back. "I hoped the massage helped?"

"Oh, absolutely. Now we'll have to see how the rest goes," she whispered the last part.

"I'm sure everything will turn out fine, Melissa." Of course, I had no way of knowing how it would go. I gave her the Thanksgiving Day plans and my address. "We'll look forward to you joining us tomorrow. I've got to go now, but please, feel free to relax for as long as you need."

I grabbed my purse and Shadow from the office. Of course, my dog ran straight to Melissa before I could stop her.

"Ugh! I *hate* slobbery dogs," I heard her mutter as I caught up to Shadow and grabbed her harness, clipping on the leash.

"Sorry, Mrs. Barnstead. We're leaving."

On the way out, I felt skeptical about people who had such reactions to animals. *Especially Labradors.* Then, I had to wonder how that'd go if she actually showed up for Thanksgiving dinner. *Ugh, why had I opened my mouth and invited her?*

I loaded Shadow into the back of my 4Runner and then pulled out my phone and dialed JJ. His voice came through the speakers as we drove out of the parking lot.

"Hey JJ…"

"Libby, just the person I wanted to talk to. I know you're super busy this week, but can you let me know when you have a few minutes?"

"I do right now."

"Great. Can you come by the station?"

"Sure, I'm not far away. But I have Shadow with me. Can she come in?"

"Yeah, no problem. Meet me at that side entrance."

"Yep, I know the one—we'll be there in ten minutes."

On the drive over, I dialed Greg.

"It's not good, Libby. Your mom's insurance company confirmed she shouldn't have paid them anything. When we called the restoration company, they knew nothing about it. A representative from there and the insurance company came by the house this morning to confirm what your mom told them. Of course, Julia recognized them as those being the ones you both met the other day. But, the crazy part—neither company sent anyone to do any work at the house this week. They confirmed it wasn't their crew that your mother gave her money to."

"What? Oh my God… who was it then?"

"Isn't that the fifty-thousand-dollar question? We've called the police."

"Oh wow."

"And what's even more heartbreaking is that they did way more damage tearing down walls yesterday. And it appears it was all just for show—and probably a method to bring immediacy for getting that payment. What a scam.

Hey, the cops just pulled up. Gotta run."

He hung up, and I sat for a couple more minutes in the parking lot at the police station, trying to process it all. *What in the world was going on? Why now?*

JJ met us at the side door and walked us to his office. Shadow sniffed her way right to his desk and it just so happened that he had treats in there.

"I keep them for the K9 unit. That way I get those furry visits each day."

I smiled at my friend, knowing full-well that's exactly the type of person he was.

"So, hey, I've been reviewing your neighbor's camera footage. Thank you, by the way, for prompting them to get involved. It's really helped."

"I'm surprised you are working on this. Wasn't it another team working my case?"

"True. But I believe there could be a link between the two."

My pulse quickened. *A murder connected to my house robbery?*

He saw my look of concern. "Oh, well, I didn't mean someone could be out to murder you, Libby. Sheesh, you turned white as a sheet." He chuckled, pulling out a chair for me. "Please have a seat."

"How are they linked, then?"

"I'm still waiting for the owner information on that van, but I'm fairly confident it's related to the Barnsteads property manager. And, in a new twist, it might be connected to a known theft ring. My best guess—it appears the deceased found herself in the wrong place at the wrong time."

He scrolled through camera footage from my neighborhood and from the Barnsteads' rental unit. He was right. The van was a similar make and model in both sets of footage. At the rental unit, over a course of months, we saw Tiago come and go, presumably maintaining the place. There were various tenants who also came and went through the front door. We watched the sixty-something couple, who were the last renters prior to the Lawsons showing up. We also saw Kaya's cleaning crew come around, also presumably doing their job cleaning, and proving the point that someone *had* cleaned after the previous tenants left and before the Lawsons arrived. However, the footage only showed a light-colored van driving out on the street and it wasn't super clear.

I was a little surprised to see a couple of large men, same build as Tiago, on the cleaning crew. That was probably my bias, though, imagining the cleaners as being an all-female crew. Nothing we saw through the rental unit cameras looked out of line or irregular. I commented how I thought it all appeared as a normal course of business, considering Tiago was the property manager for the rental property. Perfectly explainable.

We continued by reviewing the various cameras' views in my neighborhood and I felt a twinge of fear seeing a white van slowly driving through my cul-de-sac. It certainly looked like someone casing the area. Why? And was this the same van we saw in the other footage? It was the same make and model, but I now understood how the detectives would have a difficult time with reading the plates. None of the shots were clear. Hopefully, with some of their fancy computer gadgetry, they'd be able to zoom in and clear that up.

He looked away from the video screen and over at me. "Anyway, we're also still learning more about the deceased. I'm certain we'll find a connection."

"What is the latest on Carol Linton?"

JJ gasped; his head tilted as he questioned me. "Libby, how'd you know her name?"

My eyes flew open, realizing with everything that had happened, I never had that conversation with JJ.

"Um. Well, you see…"

"Libby! You can't withhold information from me."

"I know, I know." I squirmed in my chair, trying to find the right words. "There's just been too much going on this week. I completely forgot. I'm sorry."

"Forgot what? Who leaked this information? It hasn't been in the news—we've been very careful to *not* let it out."

"Then you need to have a conversation with Melissa Barnstead. That's how I learned the lady's name and who knows who else she's told."

JJ ran a hand over his closely cropped blonde hair. "Jesus, Libby!" he let out with a rush of breath. "You promised to stay away from her."

I sat up straighter in my chair. "Well, in fairness, that was before you gave me that warning."

"How long have you been holding out on me, then?"

"Well, I don't think that's what's important right now. But you should give her the warning about her loose lips."

His stare unnerved me before he finally shook it off. "Okay, I'll have a talk with her. Anyway, yes, Carol Linton is quite a mystery herself. There's very little information out there about her. But we have found her family—husband and two young children. Such a tragedy."

"A husband? What have you learned there?"

He looked at me questioningly.

"Those closest … you know, they're generally the culprit," I prodded him.

"Right. We're also closely scrutinizing him because we've learned that they recently became estranged. He moved out of their family home only a couple months back."

"Does he have an alibi?"

"He does. We're investigating whether there are any holes in it, though. He had the kids with him—but that doesn't mean he hadn't slipped out for a while."

"Did either of them live in the area near the rental?"

"No, that's what's really odd. The family home is out in Litchfield—complete opposite side of town from here."

"And where did he move to? You said he moved out…"

"Oh, essentially the same neighborhood—only a couple of miles away from the family."

"So, why was she in Mesa?"

"Exactly. That's what we'd like to know."

"And why do you think the murder could be connected to what you called a theft ring?"

He leaned back in his chair, throwing his head back, looking at the ceiling. When he leaned forward again, he pointedly looked me in the eye. "I guess I have nothing concrete. Except, there's *something* about this Santos family. But mostly it's only a hunch at this point."

"What's the connection between the Santoses and the Lintons?"

"I'm still trying to figure that out."

I sat back in my seat, considering all he'd divulged. Then I remembered the session I'd finished with Melissa and decided since I was already in trouble with JJ, I might as well go for it. "Have you heard that Fred Barnstead is cheating on his wife?"

JJ's hand slapped the desk with frustration. "How could you possibly know that?"

Then he nodded and in unison, we both said, "Melissa."

"That woman—I'm going to…"

"She was venting to me during a massage session…"

"What? I specifically asked you not to…"

"I know! Long story, but yes, I worked on her this morning. She's devastated to have learned her husband cheated on her."

JJ scoffed. "Multiple times."

It was my turn staring at him inquisitively. *Had Fred admitted to it?* "She suspects Tiago's wife. Hey, actually, maybe that's your connection?" I waited for a reaction, and when he didn't give me one, I connected the dots. "Oh, wow, do you think he was using their rental properties as places to hook up with women?"

His eyebrows lifted, indicating I might be on to something. "I really can't discuss the details—especially because you stay in contact with Melissa."

"Trust me, I've got plenty on my plate right now without her crying to me. But why is it such a problem?"

"Perceptions. I don't want to taint this investigation, and I'm trying very hard to remain unbiased. Until we completely rule out Fred and Melissa Barnstead as suspects, being the owners of the home where a woman was found dead, you and I can't have that discussion."

"Sure. Or, the other way to look at it, I might be able to gather information *for* you."

"Exactly how you could get me into trouble, Libby. Let us detectives do that work."

I felt my face flush. Admonished again.

CHAPTER SIXTEEN

By the time Shadow and I made it back home, I found the Lawson group had beat me there. Including Larry. Setting down my purse and Shadow's leash on the entryway table, I let go of Shadow and she bolted right over to the kids.

Larry, sitting at the far end of our sectional sofa, had his right leg in a large boot with it propped up on a chair. When he turned toward me, I saw bandages covered a largely bruised face. I was not expecting that. Neither was I expecting the brilliant smile that emerged next. I walked right over, standing beside him at the end of the couch.

Not sure what didn't hurt on him, I gently laid my hand on his shoulder. "Larry, how are you doing?"

"I guess as well as expected. At least I'm out of that

hospital now. No, I'm more grateful I'm off that mountain!"

"So are we! You gave us all quite the fright. I've only heard a portion of the story. Have they caught those thugs yet?"

He shook his head. "I wish."

"Any idea who they were or what they wanted?"

Larry gave a slight shrug. "I definitely was in the wrong place at the wrong time."

"Did you witness something you shouldn't have?"

"Honestly, everything keeps coming in bits and pieces..." His eyes cast upward toward the ceiling, struggling to remember. As the story poured out, we learned Larry intended to take an easy sunset hike along the base of the mountain. He said he only really wanted to watch the mountain change colors, but set out from Greg's place because he wanted to reach a slightly higher elevation, so he had city views as well.

"I trudged up a steep incline to get that view, rounding a bend in the trail, when I spotted three men huddled together, their voices hushed. Intuition warned me to turn back, but I guess curiosity got the better of me."

He approached cautiously, his eyes scanning the men for signs of trouble. Two of them wore worn-out backpacks, while the third was clutching something in his hand. By now, shadows obscured their faces, but Larry sensed the undercurrent of tension. He ventured a "Hello there," hoping to break the silence.

The men turned to face him, their eyes narrowing. One stepped forward, his voice low and menacing. "Mind your business." Larry said he saw something that looked like a metal rod in his hand—could have been a crowbar. The other two stood tall together, creating a barrier between Larry and the trail he'd been following.

Larry felt a chill run down his spine and had tried to explain simply. "I'm just passing through," he stammered, backing away. "I didn't mean to intrude."

Before he could turn and run, the man with the crowbar lunged at him. Larry ducked and stumbled backward, tripping over a loose rock. As he fell, he grabbed a large, jagged stone and hurled it at the attacker. The stone struck the man in the chest, knocking him to the ground.

Seizing the opportunity, Larry scrambled to his feet and bolted down the trail, his heart pounding. He didn't look back until he was out of sight, and the men's shouts faded behind him. Larry's panic grew, not knowing how long he could outrun them. Frantically, he searched for the trail that led him back to Greg's place. However, it was too late. He'd gone much farther than he'd realized, past the state park, and nowhere in sight of the housing developments.

He kept climbing, keeping alert for the three men who'd assaulted him. Reaching in his pockets, his phone was nowhere to be found. Voices penetrated the darkness. Panicking, he scanned the surrounding desert landscape for possible hiding spots. The only way was up, so, despite his aching legs, he scrambled up the rocky mountainside despite.

The men must have been more familiar with the terrain; they closed the gap between them and Larry. Shouting threats, their voices echoed through the canyon, determined to catch up to him. As Larry continued his ascent, the three men, fueled by anger over their earlier encounter, pursued him.

* * *

His hand rubbed his right leg and he gave a shiver. He let out a pent-up breath and knocked on his forehead with his knuckles, struggling to remember more.

"After hiding out behind a large boulder for a while, I decided it was clear, and I ventured out to find the trail. I suppose that was my last mistake. It was exactly what they were waiting for. They pounced—and even though I can't remember much after that point—I'll never forget the wild, manic intensity from the bulkiest one of them. Clearly, at some point, I went unconscious. I'm not even sure when I broke my foot. But, regardless, here I am now." He shuddered again, pointing at the black medical boot on his leg.

Bewildered, all I could do was shake my head, worried about Greg's brother. "I can't believe that. Why would anyone beat up some random stranger for no reason? I'm so sorry you went through all that, Larry."

Bill chimed in, "Maybe next time he'll stick closer to the family and follow the plans we already had in place. Who goes hiking alone near dark?"

Anne touched her husband's arm. "C'mon, Bill. He's been through enough."

Larry rolled his eyes and I caught a similar exhausted expression from Dana.

"Are you all hungry? We could order some food in, or go somewhere?"

The kids screeched, running over, begging me to choose pizza. Larry said he didn't want to move from his spot at all. Bill didn't act excited about the pizza suggestion, but acquiesced when everyone else thought it sounded great. Greg took charge of ordering and we decided on pickup versus delivery so we could have a few moments alone together.

As soon as we closed the Tundra's doors in our driveway, I began telling Greg all about the visit with Melissa earlier, my conversation with JJ, and I asked him to take the long way out of the neighborhood so we could pass by the Santos home.

He slowed as we approached, and I pointed out which place was theirs.

"Wow, fancy—it's gorgeous. And he's a property manager for the Barnsteads?"

I nodded, scanning the entire property, looking for anybody at home.

"Maybe we should be property managers, then? They make a lot of money. Look at that boat in the side yard there. That's *huge*."

"I think there's suspicion of criminal activity with the Santoses."

"How so?"

"I'm not really sure. JJ wouldn't give me specifics, but they've got them in their crosshairs."

"Really?"

I nodded.

Greg grunted and I suggested we keep moving before we were noticed on camera.

"There's way more to the story. JJ suspects that Kaya's cleaning…"

Greg interrupted. "Who's Kaya?"

"Tiago's wife. Tiago is the property manager—his wife has a professional cleaning company."

"Gotcha."

"So, we spotted a similar make Tundra model van in our cul-de-sac and at the Barnstead's rental, just like the one her cleaning crew drives."

"I guess that makes sense. That the van would be at Melissa and Fred's rental, right?"

"Yes, of course. But why in *our* cul-de-sac?"

"Maybe one of your neighbors uses the same company?"

I hadn't thought about the neighbors on the other side of my house, but Robin already confirmed she doesn't get help with cleaning duties. I needed to check with the other neighbor, though.

We pulled up at the pizza place, and I ran in to get the three pizzas. With my hands full, I used my hip to push as I exited through the swinging door, just as a burly man barreled through the opening. Clenching tightly to the boxes, I narrowly made it through without dropping them. *How rude!*

Greg witnessed and hurried from his truck, taking the boxes from me. "Are you okay?"

I assured him I was and stopped him from going inside to make a scene. We loaded into the truck, snapping our seatbelts into place.

"Where has chivalry gone? You'd have thought he'd see a lady with her arms full and would hold the door like a gentleman. Instead, he nearly knocks you over." Greg was still steaming as we pulled out of the parking space.

My eyes remained on the storefront when I saw the same man emerge from the building, as rushed as when he'd gone inside. Then I noticed them—Bright yellow running shoes.

Greg continued lamenting about how rude people could be, but I'd already tuned him out. *Who was this man with yellow shoes? Oh, that's silly ... many different people could have a similar running shoe. It doesn't mean he was the same one Shadow and I encountered previously.*

"Don't you think?" He turned his head toward me. "Hey, where are you? You're not even listening to me."

"Sorry. Just a little shaken, I guess." I stared out the window, wondering if we were being followed. "I think I've seen him somewhere before."

"You know him?"

"Well, no, I don't know him. I just feel like I've seen him around." My mind went back to that early morning chase. *Could he actually be the person who cased our house, or possibly came into our backyard?* I shook it off. "Oh, it's nothing. Now, what were you saying?"

We turned a few more corners and, before long, we pulled up in front of the house. As we unloaded the pizzas, I glanced over my shoulders. No cars. *I need to chill.*

Over dinner, the conversation became lively. Larry's tales from the hiking trail, and my mother's story about those who scammed her, sparked a lively conversation, with everyone giving plenty of advice all the way around. We finished the meal with everyone wanting to get back to their respective residences for the night.

On their way out, Dana asked, "How can we help you get set up tomorrow?"

So exhausted from the past several days, I wanted to do anything but organize. However, I plastered a smile on my face. "Let's plan on ten."

Larry piped up. "I thought we're going to Tucson tomorrow?"

Everyone's heads whipped around, eyes staring at him as though he'd sprouted horns. "Larry, you have a broken foot," his dad said.

"Yeah, and a walking boot. I'll be fine."

I looked at Greg with desperation. *When do we have time for a trip down to Tucson?*

"Guys, let's just see what tomorrow brings," Greg patiently ushered his family out the front door. "Larry's got some good medication in his system right now that may be clouding his judgment."

Shadow slipped by, running out the front door. I yelled out to Greg to get her at the same time I heard her start barking frantically. Standing in the doorway, I watched as Greg held onto her harness as he escorted everyone out to the street where their two vehicles were parked.

Mom walked up behind me. "It's getting to be a bit much, isn't it?"

I slowly nodded. "I'll be fine."

"You can say *no* to any plans at any time, you know?"

I nodded again. Silently, we turned to walk back inside.

"What the hell?!" The sound of a man's shouting voice echoed in our direction.

Mom and I halted. I left her there and ran down the driveway to find Greg's family staring at the SUV they'd rented. When I rounded the front end of the vehicle, I saw the problem. Glass was littered everywhere in the street.

CHAPTER SEVENTEEN

The driver's side windows were completely smashed out, and the door was standing wide open. The windshield was also bashed in, leaving the rearview mirror dangling in place.

Dana was pacing, anger seething from her. Anne and Bill moved the kids back onto the sidewalk, keeping them out of her way.

Greg tried diffusing the situation and to get Dana's attention focused on what could be done. "Can you look inside to see if anything was stolen? Try not to touch anything."

I scanned the cul-de-sac and noticed that no one was home in the houses on either side of me. *Had yellow shoes followed us after all?* I let Greg know I'd go inside and call the police to report the vandalism.

When I approached the front door, Mom showed concern. "What happened?"

I explained, grabbing my phone from my purse.

"What more could possibly happen to this family?" she asked.

"I think we need to stop asking that question, Mom." I dialed the police and described the situation. They said an officer was on the way.

"Mom, while we were eating, did you hear anything? That's an awful lot of damage for us not to hear it happen."

Mom shook her head.

"I'm surprised Shadow hadn't alerted us."

Then I remembered a ruckus she'd made while we were all chatting around the table. She'd been off playing with the kids, so naturally, I thought it was part of their play. *But was it?*

Greg's parents, along with their grandchildren, came back inside. Larry hobbled behind them, setting his bag on the floor, and then plopped himself down into his same spot on the sofa, lifting his foot onto the chair again. Shadow joined him, sitting at his good foot, and nosing inside the bag next to her.

Anne and I got the kids set up in front of the TV and before long, they'd tuned out the adults. I left the parents inside, while I joined Greg and Dana out on the street again.

Speaking softly to Greg, I asked, "When we went to get pizza—surely, we would have noticed this, right?" I pointed to all the debris on the street.

"Yes, we passed right by their car when we came back and parked in the driveway. I didn't see anything in the street."

I nodded, remembering that, too. "So, this happened since we've been home from that errand and while we were inside. Was anything stolen? Did a car hit their SUV, or...?"

"I think someone smashed the windows to get inside—now, whether that was meant to steal the car or its contents, I don't know. Dana left nothing inside the vehicle, so we're not sure what attracted the thieves."

Greg noticed the despair that washed over me. He reached out and pulled me into his arms.

"It'll be okay."

"Your mom and dad were already wanting to leave early. This will surely send them packing."

Dana interjected. "Don't worry. We can't leave the state until the police clear us."

I wondered again why they'd have to stay, but a cop car rolled up at that moment and I stood back while Greg and Dana gave the officers all the details. Looking toward the sky, clouds had moved in and darkened the full moon. Shadows cast around the neighborhood, which felt particularly spooky as we stood there. There was no movement or sound from the houses nearby, but I got the distinct feeling we were being watched. Chills crawled over my skin.

I heard Shadow bark from inside the house. Her nails scratched at the front door. I caught Greg's attention and told him I needed to go in. He nodded, and the officer didn't show any sign of wanting to question me, so I hurried away.

Opening the door slowly, I expected Shadow to bolt, so I bent forward ready to catch her harness on my way in. She backed up without challenge, but dropped something at my feet. It was a red and white paisley printed bandana.

"Whatcha got here?" I leaned over and picked it up and proceeded into the living room with her at my heels.

"Is this someone's bandana?" I collectively asked the Lawsons.

The kids' heads briefly turned away from the TV. Both said no.

Anne and Bill shook their heads.

Larry's head bobbed forward, and I realized he was asleep. When I walked around the sofa closer to him, I saw many items were strewn about from the bag he'd set on the floor next to him.

"Shadow, have you been naughty? Are you going through uncle Larry's stuff?"

Her ears moved back, now plastered to her head and looking guilty as hell. The large root beer-colored eyes cast downward. I threw the cloth on top of his bag and bent down to gather several other items and put them back inside.

"Whatcha doing?" he mumbled and stretched.

"Sorry to wake you. Looks like Shadow got into your stuff."

He leaned over to look. "That's not mine," he said, pointing to the bandana.

"Oh. There were other things she pulled out; I just assumed this was also from the bag. Maybe it belongs to Greg or Dana, though." Giving it a once over, and not recognizing it as Greg's, I slung it over the back of the sofa.

"Are they almost done out there? I really need to get some sleep."

Just then, the front door opened and Greg and his sister came in. Dana went to the guest room to call the rental company and report on the damaged vehicle. Greg filled us in on the dismal outlook law enforcement gave him. There were so many vehicle thefts and vandalism, they couldn't keep up, and rarely recovered or found the perpetrators.

Dana poked her head into the living. "Greg, do you have a street address out there at the trailer?" He nodded and left the room with her.

"Can anyone take me back to the trailer so I can go to sleep?" Larry pleaded.

Anne and Bill agreed. They were eager to leave as well and offered to drive Larry. By the time I got them out the front door, all I wanted to do was find my own bed. The children's laughter in the living room brought me back to reality, though. We still had guests. I sat on the floor next to them and tried to follow along with the show they watched.

Finally, Greg came out and said the rental company was sending a tow truck. "And after that's picked up, I'll need to drive her over to get another vehicle."

"They wouldn't deliver one?"

"Tomorrow they could, but not tonight. If we want one right away, we have to go to them."

I nodded and resigned myself to children's TV for the rest of the evening. Around ten o'clock, the tow truck came and then Greg was off with Dana and her kids. I fell into bed like a ton of bricks, falling immediately asleep.

Shadow's barking jolted me upright. The clock said one o'clock. Greg's side of the bed was undisturbed. *Where was he?*

Mom's voice penetrated the fog in my brain. "Libby! Help!"

CHAPTER EIGHTEEN

I ran down the hallway. Shadow scratched at her door, and I instantly pushed it open.

"Mom, what is it?"

She mumbled something and sat up. "What?"

"Mom, you screamed out for me. Why?"

"No, I didn't."

Shadow whined and put her front paws up on the side of her bed, reaching her neck out, trying to lick her grandmother. I sat down next to her on the bed.

"Just a bad dream?" I suggested.

She rubbed her eyes. "I don't remember. But I think I'd know if I called for you."

"Okay. Well, let's go back to sleep then." I went to the window and made sure it was secured. Nothing looked out of place.

Mom laid her head back on the pillow and closed her eyes. I pulled the door closed and turned toward the kitchen, turning on a light and glancing around the room. Everything looked in order. Walking back to the bedroom, I wondered where Greg was—*what was taking them so long?*

I found my phone and saw that he'd texted around eleven-thirty, saying they'd had to drive into Phoenix to another location for a car. Dana was unsure of the area, so she was following him out to his trailer and he'd be late. Don't wait up.

That was good enough for me. I crawled right back into bed and immediately fell asleep.

* * *

By the next morning, Shadow and I left Greg snoring away while we snuck out for a run, enjoying the crisp morning air. Behind my housing development are many hiking trails that ultimately lead to the Salt River. Although we wouldn't go as far as the river today, we ventured out to the desert trails. The sun was on the brink of rising, and the low-lying clouds created almost fog-like conditions. As much as you can achieve in the typically dry desert, anyway. A system had moved through the area overnight with the promise of more wet weather expected within the coming days.

As we dodged some puddles, about a mile into our run, I realized that the neighborhood where the Barnsteads had their rental was nearby. I urged Shadow down the next trail, which led us closer, and then we'd have to figure out our way through their neighborhood. My curiosity piqued, thinking about how the dead woman got into the house undetected in the first place. After reviewing the footage with JJ the day before, I realized I never saw Carol Linton enter the home.

We wound our way through the streets until I found the house I was looking for. Shadow pulled intently, straight to the garage doors.

"Do you smell something? What is it?" I reached down and petted her head. She glanced up at me, then pointed her nose directly at the garage.

Squinting slightly, my gaze focused on the exterior of the house, looking for small, circular devices mounted in the corners of the roofline. I raised my hand to shade my eyes from the sun and scanned along the front of the garages, all the way over to the west side corner of the home. Then I led Shadow around to the other side, which led to a front walkway to the entrance. There was one—a camera at the front door, looking down that walkway and toward the street. I turned back and realized that because of the house's positioning on the lot, you couldn't see the driveway from the front door. Tugging at Shadow's leash to get her attention, we went around the front corner of the house, back to the driveway. There were no cameras at all near the garage.

I pulled out the phone from my pocket; it was still way too early to make a phone call. Maybe I could catch up with JJ later in the afternoon, after our cooking session. Shadow let out a bark and I jumped. A man was coming around the front walkway.

"Can I help you?" he grumbled with a menacing stare.

"Oh! Uh, I'm sorry. Do you live here?" I countered, as I backed up a few steps. *Where had he come from? Inside?*

He progressed forward, and that's when I realized how large a man he actually was. Tall and muscular, but it was his dark eyes that bored right into me that frightened me most. His moves were deliberate and quiet; his presence made my skin crawl. Shadow's growl was persistent, but hadn't intimidated the stranger.

Still edging toward the sidewalk, I explained, "I thought this was my friend's house; sorry, I must have the wrong one." One good tug at Shadow's leash got her attention when I turned and ran, not risking a look back. We sprinted out of the neighborhood, down Power Road, and about another half mile home. Rounding the last corner, I finally slowed. No cars had followed us. I wheezed, trying to gain control of my breath. Shadow was on edge, full of energy, as we walked in the front door.

We found my mom and Greg chatting at the kitchen counter. Each had a mug of coffee in their hand. I could barely get the words out, but managed to tell them breathlessly that someone was at that rental home.

My mom said, "Isn't that far away?"

Greg, at the same time, added, "Isn't it still a crime scene?"

I nodded to both of them as I doctored my coffee and then sat down, pulling my phone from my pocket again. I didn't care how early it was—JJ needed to know this information.

"Hey Lexi …"

"It's pretty early, Libs … we're not cooking until ten, right? Oh wait, sorry … I picked up JJ's phone. What's going on?"

"Can I talk to JJ? I'll fill you in later, I promise."

"He's in the shower … oh wait, I just heard the water

turn off. Hold on."

I took a sip of my coffee, glancing at the two faces staring at me and wondering what the heck happened.

I heard shuffling sounds before his voice sounded. "Libby, it's awfully early."

"I know. I'm sorry. JJ—someone was at the rental house!" I explained everything. "Isn't it still a crime scene?"

"Not any longer. But no one should be there. Did you recognize him? I mean, it wasn't Fred, right?"

"Definitely not Fred." My mind wandered back to the scene. For some reason, it felt like I should have recognized him. "I think I was just so startled, plus he was a scary dude, JJ."

"Maybe part of the maintenance crew—Tiago's guys?"

"Perhaps. I asked him if he was staying there, but he never answered me. He was intimidating as all hell."

"Well, then, I'm glad you got out of there. I'll have an officer drive by, check it out. We'll call the Barnsteads and see if they know anything."

"Thanks! That'll make me feel better. Oh, but hey, one thing I noticed … and you probably already have figured this out, too. There are no cameras on that house nearest the garage. Maybe that's why the front entrance camera hadn't captured Carol Linton? Did she actually enter, or exit, through the garage?"

"That's a good point. Wait a minute. Were you over there snooping around?"

"Uh, well…"

"Libby, you're going to get yourself in trouble doing that! Leave the police work up to us."

"Well, it just seems you hadn't exactly figured out …"

"Libby…"

"Okay. Gotcha. Can I talk to Lexi now?"

My friend got back on the phone and we finalized plans for when she and Joshua would head over to my house.

Once I hung up, Greg smiled. "Got in trouble again with the police, didn't you?"

I finished my coffee. "Well, maybe ... unofficially anyway."

"What were you doing several miles away?"

"Running."

Greg's expression told me he didn't buy my response.

"Well, we went running through the desert trails and just happened to come back a different way."

I fixed another cup of coffee and asked my inquisitors if they'd like omelets. We chopped a bunch of vegetables and whipped up some veggie omelets, bubbling with cheddar cheese. Afterward, I loaded the dishwasher and started it; I glanced at my watch and saw I still had time to shower and run to the grocery store.

By the time I got out of the shower, Greg kissed me and said goodbye. He was headed out to his trailer to meet up with his family. Larry was stir-crazy and still wanted to go to Tucson, injured or not. Dana and Anne wanted to help Mom and me organize, and weren't excited about a road trip. But Dana was happy to send her kids off with the guys for the day, and apparently, they hadn't objected.

Mom and I made a run over to the grocery—we still had over an hour before Dana and Anne would show up at the house.

"Let's not forget to grab more butter," she reminded me.

"I can't believe how much we've gone through already. Tis the season, huh?"

As soon as we pulled into the parking lot, I was regretting the decision to shop the day before Thanksgiving. We split the list, to divide and conquer once we stepped inside the crowded grocery store. When we discovered bare shelves, substitutions became necessary. Before we could go home, we ended up stopping at two more places to complete all the shopping we had to do.

"How many people are coming tomorrow?" Mom asked, as I opened my 4Runner's back door.

"We're close to thirty now … remember Melissa is joining us now too." I handed her a couple of the lighter bags to carry inside the house.

"Sheesh. I don't know where we're going to fit everyone," she mumbled under her breath.

Honestly, I didn't know either, but I kept thinking positive. Even if people had to eat siting on the sofa, we'd figure it out somehow.

With my hands too full, I set several bags on the ground while I fumbled for my keys. Shadow was going bonkers inside.

"Does she always get this excited when you get home?"

"Not generally."

I twisted the doorknob, pushing the door as I reached down for the grocery bag handles. The front door creaked open, revealing a scene I never expected.

I stepped inside, gasping, "What the…"

CHAPTER NINETEEN

Stepping into ankle deep water, I saw Shadow inside her crate across the room. She was frantic to get out. The once-familiar living room was now a shallow pool with all the furniture sitting in ankle deep water.

"Wait! Don't come inside, Mom!" My eyes canvassed the great room in disbelief. I stepped back outside and set my bags down again.

"Where'd all that water come from?" Mom wondered.

"I'll be right back. Stay here."

I cautiously waded through the living room, seeing a couple inches of water everywhere I looked. I unlatched Shadow's crate and tightly held her collar. She was soaking wet.

"Poor girl. What on earth happened here?" I walked

her to the garage door, opened it, and told her I'd be right back. Of course, the second the door closed, she scratched at it and continued her whining.

I stopped and listened. I could hear a hissing sound that seemed to come from the hallway. As I got closer to the bathroom, I knew precisely what had happened. I reached down at the side of the toilet to turn the valve—it snapped off in my hand and water rushed from the now unattached hose.

Running back down the hall and out the front door, I hurried to the box in my front yard and lifted the lid. Spiders and other creepy crawlies emerged, causing me to jump back, dancing around, sure they crawled up my pants. *Where was Greg when I needed him?* Shaking off, I knew there was no other choice as my home was filling with water. I knelt down in the rock landscape, reaching into the ground to find the main valve and praying all the bugs made it out of the moist darkness below. Twisting the valve with all my might, it finally loosened and turned all the way right.

I got off the ground, brushing myself off, certain that there were things crawling up my sleeves and into my clothing. Running back inside, I prayed it did the trick. As soon as I rounded the corner into the bathroom, I finally took a deep breath. No more water gushed from the hose. I walked back out the front door and crumpled to the ground in the entryway.

"What happened?" Mom asked.

"Water leak. The whole house is sitting in water…" I scooted my back up against the house for support and pulled my knees to my chest.

"Oh, dear."

"Yeah. Oh, dear." I quipped, as I dropped my head onto my crossed arms over my knees. After a moment,

I looked up at her with tears in my eyes. "Okay, I admit defeat—Let's officially cancel Thanksgiving dinner now. I can't do this anymore. I give."

She didn't know what to say. After a few more minutes of listening to Shadow scratch and whine, I pulled myself together and realized none of this gets better with age. I've got groceries to put away and water to sop up. I grunted, trying to stand. This time, I'd take off my shoes. Despite my protests, my mom did the same. Together, we trudged through the water and got the groceries to the kitchen counter.

"I believe Greg has a shop vac in the garage. I'll see what I can find."

Mom nodded. "I'll put away the groceries. Then let me know how I can help."

As soon as I opened the garage, Shadow bolted into the house and splashed through the water. Choosing not to fight that battle, I let her splash throughout the house while I chased her around with the vacuum, sucking up water and dumping it out in the front landscape.

Mom found a quiet, and dry, space by sitting in my vehicle. From there, she called all the friends from my phone, delivering the disappointing news. Hours later, I sat out at the curb, utterly defeated and exhausted.

CHAPTER TWENTY

G reg and his family pulled up to the house.
Wiping my brow with my arm, then removing the gloves I had on, I managed a smile for the group.

Dana looked around at all the rugs I'd laid out in the driveway and over the hood of my vehicle. Then her eyes found the rags airing out on the branches of a nearby tree. "Wow! You're really serious about cleaning for this dinner tomorrow, aren't you?"

"Well, we're going to have to come up with yet another plan. Dinner isn't happening in there," I stated, pointing to the front door.

"What happened?" Greg's brows furrowed.

"Water leak."

"You've got to be kidding me."

My mom piped up from the passenger-side seat. "No joke about this one. Water *everywhere*."

Greg marched into the house, followed by his parents. Larry hobbled along behind them. Dana and the kids stayed outside with my mom and me.

Our attention was diverted for a second when next door, at Robin's house, a large white vehicle with dark tinted windows drove up and parked in their garage. The door closed, and I was thankful she hadn't ventured over to question my new front yard décor.

When Greg emerged again, I saw his grim expression. "How?"

"The water line on the guestroom toilet. It wasn't only dripping out—it was *pouring* out. Mom and I were gone for a couple hours when we walked into a couple *inches* of water throughout the kitchen and living room."

Now he was pacing. "So all the water is off to the house now?"

I nodded.

"Okay. Dad and I will go to the hardware store and get another water line."

"And a valve. It broke too."

"Alright. And a valve."

Anne stepped up. "What can we do to help, Libby?"

I was so overwhelmed; it was impossible to think straight. Then I remembered poor Shadow was still in the garage. "Shadow has been confined in the garage all this time. Would you ladies, and maybe the kids too, mind taking her for a walk?"

They agreed and the kids were excited when I pointed the way to a community park. The four of them were now out of my hair and I turned to the guys.

"Greg, can you call around … maybe Lexi and JJ have some fans we could borrow? If not, check with Jordan, too. We need to get air circulating in there—I've turned on all the ceiling fans, but we'll need more."

Without hesitation, Bill and Greg got in his truck and set out to complete their tasks.

That left me with Larry, who complained he'd been on his feet too long already today. I'd noticed that while we were sorting out the next steps for everyone, he seemed to lurk, almost hiding, against the large tree in my yard.

"Mind if I go inside? I really need to put this foot up." Larry was subdued; much quieter than his normal self. His eyes darted across the street and then over to the next-door neighbor's house.

I found his behavior odd, but also, part of me wanted to smack him—*No kidding he'd need rest; they shouldn't have gone off to Tucson all day.* I pushed the negativity from my thoughts and helped him get set up on the sofa with his foot elevated again. He seemed calmer and before I knew it, his eyes were closed.

Mom came around the corner from the bedroom. "The carpet is soaked in my room—not all the way in, but maybe a couple feet."

I followed her and inspected. That reminded me to call the insurance company. Even as fast as we'd attempted sucking all the water out, I could see areas along the walls—in the bathroom, the hallway, and partially into the front entryway—where water had soaked in. The water had soaked into the carpet in the hallway and partially into each of the bedrooms. Furniture in the living room already showed water stains where it rested on the flooring.

My phone rang and I saw it was Lexi. "Hey," I answered.

"My goodness, Libby … are you okay? Your mom didn't say anything earlier, other than you were canceling. Greg just got here and JJ is giving him all the fans we've got."

"Ugh, I'm so sorry for bailing."

"Libby, don't be ridiculous!"

"It's all so much. But we've made a lot of progress cleaning. It's just musty as heck in the house, and there's so much more to be done." I explained what had happened and she listened intently. "We'll need to get this food divided up so everyone has *something* for tomorrow."

"Let me do that. I'll get with Bella, CB, and Sage … we'll handle everything. You let us know what else you need and we're there for you."

"Thank you, my friend."

When I hung up, tears stung at my eyes. *No, there's no time for crying.* I looked up the insurance company and called them. By the time I'd hung up, after being told no one would be out until Friday, Greg and Bill were back.

I followed Greg into the bathroom. "Have you done this before?"

"Oh yeah, many times. Not a problem."

Relieved, I leaned against the countertop and watched.

He muttered from the floor, "Oh hey, I saw Robin and her husband outside. That's what you said her name was, right?"

"Yeah. She's a character."

"They've got their hands full of kids, that's for sure."

"I'm surprised they were out front—she never allows them to play in the front yard. And I can understand why, after seeing one of those toddlers darting around. He'd be in traffic so fast."

"Maybe with him home, and with the extra set of hands, it helps?"

He grunted, wrenching the new hose tightly into place. After screwing on the new valve, he sat up. "Ready to test it out?"

"Are you sure it's tight? I really don't want to clean more."

He smiled. "Trust me. It'll be fine."

I had no choice. We needed water for the house. I trudged out to the water meter again, wishing I'd asked Greg to do this part, but also not wanting to admit I needed the help. Bending over, I lifted the metal cover and jumped back, watching the bugs scurry again. *Dangit, I hate bugs!* I shook it off, knelt down on the ground and quickly reached down and turned the valve, waiting for Greg to holler.

When I heard nothing, I stood and noticed Robin's family's eyes on me. I'd never met her husband before, and shrouded in a hoodie, bent over instructing one kid, I couldn't get a clear picture of him now. I just waved and shouted, "Water leak."

She started in my direction. He took the infant she offered and ushered all the kids inside the house. I met her partway, standing on the edge of my driveway.

"I was wondering, seeing all your rugs outside. Thought you were doing some spring cleaning. Only in the fall." She chuckled, amused with herself.

"Yeah, I'm not that great of a cleaner."

"Hey, have you considered hiring Kaya?"

"Maybe after all the water damage repairs are done, actually. Would be a good idea." Then, I remembered what Melissa had said about her suspicions about the lady.

Maybe I'd find another company instead.

"Are you ready for tomorrow? Didn't you say you had family in town for Thanksgiving?"

I hadn't remembered telling her that, but simply answered, "Yep, we have family here and we'll figure it out. It's quite the mess inside there."

"You know, if you want to—come join us! We'll have *plenty* of food. For you two and his family."

"Oh, aren't you so sweet. That's a very nice offer." I explained how we'd prepared so much food already for a large group and how I had to cancel that plan. "I think we'll work it out with the immediate family, but I'll suggest your offer as well and let you know. Hey, I've got to get back inside—we're right in the middle of fixing the leak."

"Sure, no problem. Let me know!"

When I walked back in the bathroom, Greg was carefully checking all connections for leaking, then he stood up. "All fixed," he declared.

I gave him a big hug. "Thank you!"

We walked into the living room. Larry had turned on the TV and was flipping through sports channels. Mom sat at the breakfast bar with her cup of tea.

"Well everyone, we've been invited to the neighbor's house for Thanksgiving."

Larry turned in his seat. His face immediately went pale. "Uh, no! I mean, we can't. It's not a good idea."

Greg and I looked at him curiously. "Um, might not be ideal, but it's not like we have a functioning household right now," Greg added. "What a nice offer."

Larry shifted uncomfortably, tugging at his shirt. "It's just … I don't think it's a good idea. Trust me."

"You don't even know them…" I added. "Or do you?"

Greg laughed. "Trust *you*? After you keep slipping off and then getting yourself hurt. We should trust *your* judgement?"

He gulped. "There's something … *off* about them."

Again, I stated, "How do you even know them?"

His eyes darted around nervously. "Well, now you've got us all curious," Greg said, crossing his arms. "What's the big secret, Larry?"

"Maybe nothing," Larry muttered, his voice barely a whisper. "Or maybe everything."

CHAPTER TWENTY-ONE

Thunder roared overhead, and I jolted. Both Greg and I reacted at the same time—the rugs outside! Rain was already coming down. He ran and opened up the garage. Together, we pulled in the area rugs and gathered the various rags from the yard before they blew away.

As the garage door was closing, I saw a figure standing in the shadowy recesses of Robin's front entryway. *Was that her husband?* The metal door clanged into its closed position before I could make out who it was.

The sound of my phone had me jump in surprise; it was Sage calling. I went inside the house, walking down the hallway toward my bedroom as I answered it.

"Libby, I'm sooo sorry to hear what happened at your house. Mercury must be in retrograde with all this disruption surrounding you—I haven't paid attention, but I need to pull out my charts." She sighed. "Listen, I want to make a proposal. We have all the food prepared, except for the turkey. I have plenty of space at my place, and it would be an honor if I could take over hosting duties. Of course, I don't want to overstep my bounds, so only if that would be of help to you. Please consider it."

"Sage. Wow! Really?" Tears sprang to my eyes as the weight of the day collapsed me onto the bed. "That's an awful lot to take on. You realize the guest list had increased to around thirty people, right?"

"Sure, it's a sizeable crowd. So, no better place than here where I have an acre and a half of space!"

She was right, her place would be perfect for hosting a large gathering. I felt weird about accepting such an offer; but also, I knew how genuine and overly generous my friend was. She never would have offered if she wasn't one-hundred percent willing.

"If you're absolutely certain—it would be an enormous help. I really hadn't wanted to cancel altogether. Everyone will help with the setup; we insist. We already have extra folding tables and the chairs—we've got everything we'll need."

"Exactly. See, I won't have to do a thing." She laughed and then we made a plan for us to head out there with all the necessities.

"Okay, I'll get my mom back on the phone with everyone to let them know about Plan … where are we at now, *Plan D*?" We both had a good chuckle.

It was raining buckets by now, and when I walked into the living room, I noticed the kids were glued to the TV. Dana, Anne, and my mom were conversing over tea at the breakfast bar. Bill and Greg examined the plywood on the back sliding door.

"It's holding up, right?" I asked the guys at the door.

"Yeah, it looks good. Don't worry." Greg pulled me into another hug. "Is Sage okay with the cancellation?"

"Actually, we have a new plan. Plan D!"

Larry shifted in his seat again. All the voices in the room ceased and they turned to stare at me.

"Sage wants to host us at her house. The *entire group*."

Larry let out a visible sigh of relief.

Dana asked, "Isn't her house right next to where we're staying at Greg's trailer?"

"That's right. Easy!"

Everyone seemed content with that plan and mom jumped right into action when I asked her to get on the phone and communicate Plan D to the others.

I turned to my partner and his father. "Wanna help transfer tables, chairs, and food to Sage's house?"

Dana spoke up. "I can help, too. We can load the food into our SUV. I'm sure the kids and Larry would like to get back to the mountain."

Larry scoffed. Given a choice, I thought Larry would rather be a permanent fixture on our sofa for the afternoon. As soon as I had that thought, he moved, groaning as he stood.

The windshield wipers worked overtime, swiping sheets of rain from our view. I'd remembered hearing there was a storm coming, but I had no idea it would be this intense. As we made our way from Mesa into Apache Junction, the streets were already pooling with water. The farther down Lost Dutchman Trail we traveled, the puddles turned to massively flooded streets. We wound our way through neighborhoods, trying to find a safer route.

Dana followed behind us, tentative and appearing to lose traction several times. I commented to Greg to slow down to make sure she was able to keep up.

"I can only imagine Larry's commentary as a backseat driver—she must be out of her mind," Greg mentioned.

I agreed. "I am glad he rode with her, though."

Finally, we made it into Sage's neighborhood.

"Whoa!" Greg said. "Look at all this water."

All the roadside ditches, as well as the normally dry washes, had rushing water in them. The usual fifteen-minute drive to Sage's took us over forty. We backed up to her garage and quickly unloaded where she instructed us to. Then Dana took Larry and her kids over to the trailer, leaving Greg and me to visit with Sage.

"Whew! This storm…" I said, shaking out my drenched hair. Everyone backed up a few steps when Shadow shook water everywhere.

She nodded. "Yeah, the rain should be out of here overnight. Crossing fingers—hopefully those forecasters are right."

"Do these tables go on your back patio?"

"Yeah, but let's just them leave here until morning. Here, c'mon inside. Let's get the food in the refrigerator."

I glanced at Shadow, then back to Sage. "Are you sure?"

"Of course! She's always welcome, you know that."

We each grabbed casserole dishes and tote bags with food containers in them and walked through the door into her large kitchen. As I scanned the room, all my previous worries melted. This space was going to work out well, and so much better than at my place. She placed things as she wanted them in the refrigerator and then we walked over to her back glass French doors, looking out upon her vast covered patio and backyard. Sheets of water were pouring off the roof and patio cover, creating streams that pooled farther out, closest to the fencing.

"Yeah, we'll have the guys set up the tables and chairs in the morning. We're going to have to sweep too. How about you guys and Lexi's family plan on coming over about eight?"

"Are you sure you're up for that? We don't *have* to keep the same schedule we'd planned for at my house."

"Oh, no ... I want to do everything the way you intended. And that should be plenty of time since we've told everyone to show up at nine. And, you know how it is with this group, everyone will pitch in and help."

Greg shook his head in confusion. "Wait, why are we starting this party so early?"

Both Sage and I started counting off using our fingers. "The parade, *lefse*, appetizers, dog show, the main meal, and football later on, of course. There's a big day ahead!"

Greg questioned, "Lef...?"

Sage explained about Cody and Brad's contribution and how we're going to make a breakfast of it. I still don't think he understood why we'd be out here the entire day, but he was up for anything. It didn't matter.

"Oh shoot, I forgot the cute turkey centerpieces for the tables. I better start making another list." I pulled out my phone to jot some notes and realized it was nearly four o'clock already. "Since we're not setting any of this up now, we should probably get back. We left my mom there running the communications end of this operation."

Sage smiled. "Yeah, I think with all the meal preparation

we've done ahead of time, we're perfectly fine. When you get here in the morning, we'll start cycling casserole dishes through the oven. I have plenty of food warmers—we'll set them up over there on the buffet. No worries at all."

I reached over and pulled her in for a tight hug. "You've saved Thanksgiving. I truly appreciate you."

She walked us back out through the garage and we ran to the truck, trying to avoid getting any wetter. Before Greg started the engine, he turned to me.

"I think I'll go hang with the family. Why don't you take my truck and I'll get Dana to bring me home later."

"You want her out driving those streets again?"

"I'm sure it'll ease up soon."

We drove next door to his trailer, and I hopped into the driver's seat as he ran inside. Leaving the neighborhood, and seeing all the washes swollen with water, I prayed it would ease up real soon.

CHAPTER TWENTY-TWO

I pulled up into our cul-de-sac and remembered Robin's invitation. Once parked in my driveway, I picked up my phone and scanned it for her phone number. Several scrolls through my contacts confirmed I didn't have her number. Looking into the backseat, two large brown eyes stared at me like, *what's taking so long—let's go!*

"Okay, we'll run over there really quick," I said to Shadow.

The rain wasn't coming down as hard in Mesa for the time being, but it still hadn't stopped. I unloaded Shadow, clinging to her leash. We bolted from the truck, crossed over the gravel that bordered the two driveways, and up to the neighbor's front patio. I could already hear the ruckus inside their house as we approached. I couldn't help but grin; Sage would never know what a savior she truly was.

The second the door chimed, I heard the roar from the other side. "Robin! Get the door!"

"Can't you?" Her voice sounded in return. Then, as she swung open the door, her grimace changed to a bright smile. In her sweetest voice, she greeted me. "Why, Libby! What are you doing out in that rain?" She looked down at the dog, and then ushered us inside. "Please, get out of the cold. C'mon in."

We stepped just inside and I held Shadow even closer when three of the littles came barreling down the hallway. I saw a bulky man with dark hair sitting in a recliner in the living room, but he made no move to come greet us. Although, I heard some muttering about *wet dog*.

"I would have called, but figured out I didn't have your number," I started. "Are you sure it's okay to have her in here?" I pointed to Shadow.

"Oh yeah, no problem," she said distractedly, as she pulled her phone from a pocket and said, "What's your number?"

As I rattled it off, she punched buttons and a nanosecond later said, "There, you have mine now, too!" The squeal she let out reminded me of how high school cheerleaders geared up a crowd. With that, I swore I heard another grumble come from the other room.

"Anyway, I wanted to thank you again for your earlier offer about Thanksgiving dinner. It was so kind of you." I explained to her about our group plans and how they'd changed. She looked heartbroken. "But let's all get together soon. I'm sure it will be a much better visit after the hustle and bustle of holidays, anyway."

Before she could respond, two of the older kids were wrestling around and then there was a loud shriek before their dad's booming voice hollered, "Shut up!"

I visibly startled. Robin looked mortified. Then, turning back to me, she muttered, "I understand." At that moment, Arlo launched over onto Shadow, trying to climb on her like a horse.

My arm automatically went out to block, only I dropped the leash at the same time. Shadow became so excited about playing that she turned quickly, knocking the child over. Arlo filled the house with a blood-curdling scream that stunned all of us, including Shadow. I quickly grabbed her leash before she got away and picturing her lapping their home with the zoomies.

"Is he okay?" I attempted to ask Robin over the ear-piercing shrieks.

"He'll be fine," she began.

I felt her husband's large presence looming over us, wanting to know what happened. Gasping when I saw his face, I'd seen him before. I was certain of it. Shadow pulled at me and I accidentally dropped the leash again. Bending over to grab at her, I managed to kick several shoes from a pile inside the doorway. My heart lurched when I picked up a pair of yellow trainers. I looked up at the man who was glaring down at me, only to quickly return to straightening up the pile of shoes. As I did, something metallic hit the tile. I picked it up—it was a lock.

Holding it in my hand, turning it and inspecting it closer, I swallowed hard. It had been cut and wasn't functional. "Hey! This is the same type of lock I had on my gate," I said, handing it to Robin. "Did you happen to find this out front somewhere?"

She glanced at her husband, Archie. He whisked it out of her hand and coldly said, "No, it's ours."

My head was spinning. *What do I do?* It seemed like too much of a coincidence. However, the brawny man terrified me. I simply nodded, only wanting to get home. "Well, Robin, we should go. Are you sure Arlo is okay?"

"Oh, yes. He's a handful." She looked wistfully at me. "I'm sorry you won't be joining us tomorrow." I felt terrible for her.

"I'm sorry, but we'll get together soon. Let's make it happen." I found myself saying the words as everything in me screamed to get out of their house.

Turning for one last glance at the family standing in the doorway as we walked away, I'd never forget his eyes leering at me. We took off across the driveway, but I couldn't help myself when I saw their side yard gate. Out of the view now from the front door, I led Shadow over to the gate and reached over, feeling for the clasp. There was a lock in place on their gate.

My brain seemed to scream. *Liar!* Then movement caught my attention through the wooden slats. I leaned in with one eye closed, peering into the gap, when I startled and stumbled backward. Archie was staring through, making direct eye contact with me. Shadow barked, and I immediately pulled her as I ran to our front door.

Fumbling for my keys, I dropped them and popped down, picked them up and clumsily slid the key into the lock and twisted. Pushing the door in, I dropped Shadow's leash and it trailed behind her as she whooshed past me.

I grappled with my phone, nearly dropping it several times as I made my way to my bedroom, but finally found the right contact and pushed the button.

C'mon, JJ! Pick up!

It went to voicemail. Then I had a horrifying thought

of Archie coming over to confront me. I ran down the hallway and double checked the front door—whew, I had locked it. I checked each window and prayed the plywood in the back doorway would hold.

Then I bolted to my mom's room and found that she was resting in her room.

"Hey, Libby. I thought I heard you come in. I'm just so tired."

"Are you okay?"

"Oh yeah. It's just been several long stressful days."

"Yep, I definitely hear that. Hey, Mom, please don't answer the door if someone knocks, okay?"

"Why?"

Not wanting to go into much detail and stressing her further, I only said, "Just don't. Promise me."

She pushed herself up to sit and then swung her legs over the side of the bed. "What's going on, Libby?"

"I need to consult with JJ first, but I had a strange interaction with my neighbors just now. Well, specifically, the man of the house. Please stay clear of him."

"Okaay." She appeared skeptical, but at least she agreed. "Shall we get some tea?"

I nodded, and we went to the kitchen. Despite all the fans still being powered on high, the horrible musty smell permeated the room. The storm wasn't exactly helping remove humidity.

"We should probably pick up some dehumidifiers." Mom picked up on me sniffing the air.

"Yeah, that's a good idea. I'm so exhausted, though. I really don't want to go anywhere and the streets are a mess right now, too."

"Greg didn't come back with you?"

"No, he'll have Dana drive him home later."

The crack of thunder startled us both. Then an eerie quietness descended upon the house. We'd lost power.

"Well, that's just great." I checked my phone to see if JJ had responded to my text. No reply yet.

"We'll be fine. They're generally good about restoring power quickly around here."

"I know. It's just that I really need to talk to JJ."

Another flash, followed by a long rumble of thunder that shook the house. Shadow shifted closer, sitting on my feet.

"Are you getting hungry?" Mom asked.

"Not really. But I'm ready to be done with this day." I looked over at the electric oven, wishing we had gas instead.

Out of the quietness, a loud banging sounded at the front door.

Mom and I stood in the dimly lit kitchen, our faces drawn tight with worry. The knock came again, louder this time. Three sharp raps.

My mother's eyes went wide. "Oh, no. It's him, isn't it? The awful man from next door." Her voice trembled.

"Okay, let's stay calm," I whispered, swallowing hard. "Let me check."

I moved slowly, peeking through the peephole, only to see a shadowy figure standing on the porch. My heart thudded in my ears. "I can't see who it is; he's turned away from me," I whispered. "Just standing there."

I turned back to my mom. She wrung her hands. "What could he possibly want?"

The knocking turned into a heavy pounding, and they both jumped.

"Go away!" I called out, my voice shakier than I'd

intended. "We're not interested."

There was a pause, and then a voice came from the other side of the door; deep and authoritative.

"Libby! It's JJ! Open the door, please."

Relief washed over as I cautiously opened the door only a crack. Sure enough, it was my detective friend with his dark hooded rain jacket on.

"Oh, thank goodness!" I invited him inside.

"What's going on?"

My mom let out a tremendous sigh. "We thought you were…"

JJ's head moved back and forth between the two of us. "Thought I was *who*? Why are you so afraid?"

"Come on in—I have so much to tell you."

He took off his wet jacket and hung it up on the coat rack in the hallway before following us into the kitchen, where we sat at the table.

"I'd offer you tea or coffee, but the power just went out."

"No worries. Yeah, this storm is a doozy!" He pulled out a chair and took his seat. "Hey, your messages sounded frantic. What's up?"

I was several sentences in, explaining what I'd seen: Archie, the shoes, and the lock. His eyes widened and after a second or two, the only thing he muttered was, "It has to be connected. I had a feeling."

CHAPTER TWENTY-THREE

Mom and I stared at JJ, waiting for more details. My friend sat contemplating for a few more minutes before asking me to start over and tell him everything from the beginning. The first time I saw the yellow-shoe man, and any suspected subsequent sightings—he wanted all the details.

While I was recounting the past week's events, I suddenly remembered the run-in with a man of Archie's stature who was leaving the police station the day the Lawsons were interviewed. I couldn't be certain he was the same man, but as JJ said, everything I could remember was important. I recalled being spooked, even feeling as though he had followed me to my mother's home, but also recounted how I'd seen him walk to another building next to the police station.

"What businesses are in that building next door to your office?" I asked him. "That's where he went that day. It might tell us something."

JJ thought for a second. "Lawyer offices. More parking."

"Hmm. What does this tell us? Do you think it was my neighbor who broke into my home and destroyed it? Seriously? And *why*?"

Mom remembered something. "JJ—Libby said you were going over to the Santos household. What did you learn?"

"Oh, right. So, this whole time, I'd been fairly certain Tiago and his wife knew nothing about the incident at the Barnstead's rental. However, the van caught on neighbors' cameras was still confounding us. We don't have clear pictures and hadn't positively identified the owner of the vehicle, but I went over to their home today hoping to see the van for myself."

"And did you see it?"

He nodded. "It was sitting right out in front of the house when I got here. It's definitely *not* the van seen in any of the footage. As you would recall, on camera, we only saw a solid white van. Kaya's cleaning crew van has a business logo wrap that encases the entire vehicle."

I felt my spirits deflate. "When you arrived here today, though, it seemed there was something more substantial that you had discovered. What was that?"

He sat up straighter and smiled. "Even though I believe the patriarch of the family could be innocent, I hadn't considered his adult sons."

I thought back to my conversation with Robin and remembered how her kids had playdates with the Santoses kids. "Oh, I was under the impression they had school-aged children."

"That's right; he and Kaya do. However, Kaya is Tiago's second wife—and much younger than his first. He has three sons with his first wife. They are in their late twenties or early thirties—my best guess, anyway."

"And now you suspect them?"

"While I was over there talking to Tiago and his current wife, two of them barged on in the house like they owned the place."

"Do they live there?"

"No. And I caught Kaya's displeasure with them. There's definitely friction." He cleared his throat. All three of us heard the wind pick up and heard the plywood creaking with movement at the backdoor. "Anyway, more so than their appearance in the room was what I overheard them saying before they realized they had an audience. One said to the other, something like 'he'll never talk, don't be stupid, and it's only oxy.' And then a third man, unrelated to these two, came through the door saying, and I paraphrase, 'doesn't matter; I took care of him.' I've been in this business a long time now—Tiago's sons are up to something."

"And you think it's related to the theft in the neighborhood? Or?"

"Oh! That's the other thing! The autopsy results came back. It's confirmed that Carol Linton had drugs in her system. But that's not the only thing—there were signs of asphyxiation, strangulation."

"Oh wow. Poor lady. Has her husband's alibi stood up?"

"We're still investigating, but so far, yes. My theory

about the Santos boys is that they are part of a drug ring. I don't have concrete proof yet, but I believe if I follow that line, we'll find our suspect. The one who killed Carol."

"Do you still believe that her death could have a connection to the theft in this neighborhood?"

He shook his head. "I'm leaning toward them being two separate incidents now."

"And any update on Larry's assault?"

"None."

"So, where do we go from here?" I was particularly bothered because Yellow Shoes, *my neighbor*, had lied to me about the gate lock. I was certain that one was mine— stolen when he was in my backyard. The thought sent chills down my spine. "Are you going to talk to Archie next door?"

"I can try. Really, you should update the officers on that case—you filed a report when the break-in happened, right?"

I nodded. My eyes pleaded for his help, though.

"Well, I suppose I could pop over when I leave here. It would be good to see what kind of reaction he has, anyway." He pushed his chair back to stand up. "Hey, tomorrow's the big day and I hear we're headed to Sage's home. I can't wait to see inside her place—from the outside, it's stunning."

He paused for a moment, staring at a pile on a nearby chair. "Where'd you get this?"

I looked at the gray cloth he held up. "Not sure. Think Bella found it when we were cleaning up after the break-in. She helped fold blankets, towels, and random rags we found. Those thieves really went through everything!"

"Hmm ... looks familiar. I've seen these somewhere before. Maybe Lexi buys the same brand of rags."

I walked him to the door, filling him in on our latest plan and thanking him for talking to the neighbors. Feeling much more confident now after his visit, I only wished now for the power to come back on.

Greg called about an hour later. He reported that the roads were completely flooded and the rain was still going strong. There was no way out until the rain ceased. I updated him on my afternoon, giving the rundown on the interactions with the neighbors. He didn't like that and was thankful that JJ had come by and also that he said he'd talk to them.

"Keep the doors locked. With this storm—you two need to stay inside, anyway."

"At some point, I've got to take Shadow out. There's no way to the backyard."

"Oh crap, I forgot about that. Well, if you go out front, carry that handheld taser I bought for you."

"I really don't think he'll do anything. JJ helped to calm me down."

Greg paused, saying nothing more on that. I got the message—carry my taser. He was such a protectionist.

When he spoke again, he lowered his voice. "Hey, I learned more from Larry, by the way."

"Oh yeah?"

"It's too close quarters here right now," he whispered. "I'll have to fill you in later. Let's just say that he's not completely innocent in his assault."

"What?" That shocked me. "Did he pick up on some man's woman or something?"

He chuckled. "No, nothing like that. Listen, can't talk right now."

"Dang it—I want the gossip!"

"Later. As soon as this rain stops, I'll get Dana to drive me home. I just wanted you to know that we're stuck here for now. We'll scrounge something up for dinner here—you and your mom do the same. I'll see you soon."

"Love you!" We hung up, and then I remembered I never told him the power was out.

Mom was already milling through the fridge when I came back into the kitchen. "Might as well use stuff up before it goes bad. What if they don't get the power back on until tomorrow?"

"I could eat now … what do we have?"

"Too bad you took all the Thanksgiving stuff over to Sage's earlier. Those pigs-in-a-blanket would have been good. Nobody would have noticed a few missing." She bent to see the bottom shelves and pulled out a container. "Here are some leftovers from a few days ago—Chinese food?"

"Sure—sounds good." Then I reminded her we'd be eating it cold. No microwave. No electric stovetop. "Maybe sandwiches and chips tonight?"

She started pulling out bread, lunchmeat, cheese, and mayonnaise. Shadow whimpered at my feet.

"You think you get dinner, too?" I chuckled, teasing her. "Of course, I'll get you some food." She wiggled and whined until I set her full bowl down on the floor in front of her.

An enormous gust of wind made the whole roof creak. Each of us craned our necks, looking at the ceiling. The rumbling of thunder and the continuous sound of rain beating down only made me want to curl up in bed and sleep through it all. My muscles ached from exhaustion.

We ate our cold sandwiches, sitting in the stuffy closed-up house, watching darkness descend. I found battery-operated candles, and we set them out in each room as well as carrying flashlights too. Soon, we couldn't hold our eyes open much longer. Conversation had run out, and we each went to our bedrooms. The storm would pass. Greg would be home soon. At least that's what I kept telling myself.

CHAPTER TWENTY-FOUR

Curled up in my bed, I pulled out my phone and checked to see if Carol Linton had an Instagram account. I figured this would help occupy my mind instead of listening to the storm and obsessing over whether it'd blow the roof off.

Scrolling through several people with the same name, but who lived in different states, I finally found one who lived in Litchfield, AZ. I had no idea what the woman looked like, but after scrolling through some of her publicly shared photos, I thought it had to be her. Despite the divorce, I found it surprising to see that she shared photos with her husband in them. But those also included various family vacations with her two children, so I guess that made sense. My heart was heavy for the kids now that their mom was gone.

Continuing to scroll, I got to the part of her story where she and a girlfriend of hers were on a double date. *I wonder if they interviewed that friend yet?* Their dates looked like respectable men, younger than themselves, but it appeared they were having a good time. I kept scrolling. My eyelids felt heavy, and I nearly dropped the phone several times.

Then I sprang up. I scrolled back to the previous photo. I swore it looked like … *Fred?* Zooming in on the photo, it was unmistakable. Melissa Barnstead was right. *Oh, no! Fred's connected to this woman… could he have? NO!*

I immediately dialed JJ. He didn't answer. I checked my watch—it was only ten, so not too late. Instead of dialing again, I texted and included the link to the Instagram account: have you checked out carol's insta?

Scrolling further, I saw that had been the only picture with Fred. There were plenty of photos of her with various other men, though. I was lulling myself back into sleepiness when I came across another one that got my attention. Carol wore western wear, maybe from line dancing at a bar one night. She had a red bandana around her neck and a thousand-watt smile. The selfie captured an angle that prevented me from seeing the whole person she was with, but I instantly recognized his eyes.

Terror ran through me. I tried JJ's number again; still no answer. Another text: CALL ME ASAP!

It was then that I heard glass crashing to the tile floor in another room. Shadow barked ferociously and jumped up at my bedroom door, wanting out. With my heart hammering in my chest, I strained to hear over the pounding in my ears. Sliding out of bed as quietly as I could, I reached for my phone, which I'd dropped in the bed. Slipping into the hallway and holding onto Shadow's collar, we made our way toward my mom's room. Shadow stood there, outside her room, with her ears pricked and alert.

"You heard it too?" I whispered to my dog, as I quietly opened the guestroom door.

Mom was already awake, sitting up in bed, her eyes wide. Shadow pulled away from me and went right to her side before turning her head back and growling, her eyes fixed on the door. Together, the three of us crept down the hallway, each step seeming to echo louder than the last. The living room was dimly lit by the candle we'd left on. Suddenly, a bolt of lightning illuminated the entire room for a second. I jolted, seeing the shadow of a man dressed all in black, standing along the wall across the room from us.

Julia tightened her grip on the small flashlight she'd grabbed from her nightstand. "Who's there?" she called out, her voice steady, but I could feel the tremble in my mother's hand.

The figure turned. He was tall, wearing a hood which cast his face further into darkness. For a moment, he stared back at us—those chilling black eyes.

I simply asked him, "What do you want, Archie?" Trying to keep steadiness in my voice, I put on a brave stance. For a moment, we had a silent standoff. Then, without a word, he took a step toward us.

Before either of us could react, Shadow sprang into action. With a fierce bark, she launched herself at the intruder, teeth bared. The man staggered back, clearly not expecting an eighty-pound dog to come hurtling toward him. Shadow clamped down onto the intruder's arm, growling with a ferocity I'd never heard from her before.

"Shadow, no!" Julia shouted, but also with a hint of

relief in her voice. The intruder struggled, trying to shake the dog off, but Shadow held firm, forcing him backwards.

Finally, with a desperate shove, the intruder wrenched free and scrambled out of the window he'd entered by, disappearing into the rain-soaked night. Shadow stood at the window, barking furiously until the darkness swallowed the sound of his retreating footsteps.

I stared at my mom with my mouth wide open, and both of our hearts raced. Then Julia dropped to the sofa and wrapped her arms around Shadow, her voice thick with emotion. "Good girl, Shadow. You saved us."

Banging sounded at the front door. My mom leaped up from the couch. I ran to the kitchen and grabbed the largest knife I could find.

"Are you kidding me?" I'd had enough. I lifted the butcher knife and bolted to the door. "I can't believe he'd come back—pounding on the door? The nerve!"

My mom followed behind me. I peered into the darkness through the small hole, where all my bravado melted away. "There's *two* dark figures!" I whispered to her before turning to the door and screaming, "Get out of here! I've called the police already. Leave us alone!"

JJ's voice sounded. "Libby, let me in! He's cuffed—let us in out of the rain!"

Shaking with fear, I questioned whether it was actually the detective I'd heard. Mom nodded her head. "It's him. Let him in."

I opened the door and stood back, ready to stab the intruder if he was trying to trick me. Shadow lunged, but then saw JJ and started wriggling, before growling again at the man our friend had in handcuffs. JJ pushed his suspect through the doorway and marched him right over to the kitchen table. He shoved him into a chair with the perp grunting in pain.

JJ slapped the hood off his head and, sure enough, my neighbor Archie was the culprit shrouded in all black. Shadow lunged at him again, hellbent on protecting all of us. Blood dripped down his hand and onto my floor from the earlier attack. I walked Shadow out to the garage and gave her a treat.

JJ was as angry as I've ever seen him. "What were you doing lurking around her house?" he screamed at Archie.

Mom didn't wait for the man to answer, and she told JJ, "He broke in! He broke that window!" She pointed across the room.

"How did you know he was out there?" I asked JJ.

My friend never removed his eyes from his perp as he answered me. "I told you about my earlier visit with Tiago and his wife. Well, this is the dude that walked in with Santoses sons. When I left here earlier to question him about that lock you found at his house, he'd already left. Probably with Carlos, if I had to guess."

I was stunned. "Archie knows them?"

JJ ignored my question and directed his own at the intruder. "Where were you last Thursday?"

The man twisted up his face, looking confused.

"Last Thursday! Where were you?" JJ was losing patience quickly. "Ok then, let me tell *you* my theory. You and the Santos brothers were covering up a murder, weren't you?"

My mom and I stared at each other, both mouthing, *what?*

"You didn't have time—the family showed up before you could get your lover's body out of the house, right?"

The man glared at JJ with a stone-cold face.

"Bet your wife would tell us you were on a business trip, or something of the sort, wouldn't she?" I added. "Maybe I should call and ask?"

"No! Don't call her," he quickly answered.

"What's your involvement with the murder of Carol Linton?"

"Who?"

"You didn't even know the name of the woman you killed?"

Archie's face turned white. His head fell forward. "Honestly, I only knew her first name. We'd gone on a couple of dates. That's it. That's all I know."

My eyebrows lifted. *So, it was true.*

JJ paced around the table, nudging his perp every time he passed by him. "Where did you go on this date?"

"Nowhere. I made her a lovely dinner—both of us wanted to stay in. That's it."

"No dancing? No drinking? No *drugs*?"

"We had wine—in fact, she had several glasses."

"And?"

"That's it…I swear!"

JJ got right up in his face. "Then *how* did your date *die* that night?" he screamed.

Agitated, Archie squirmed in his seat. "I have no idea!"

"I don't believe you."

The front door opened; Greg and Larry walked in.

Relieved, I ran right into Greg's arms. The embrace was short-lived when Larry tried to push past us to get back out the front door. Greg stopped him.

"I can't believe you!" Larry shouted. "*This* is why you wanted me to come with you?"

I stood back, confused. "What's going on?"

JJ stood, crossing the room. "Thank you, man." He shook Greg's hand, then took Larry by the arm and led him over to the kitchen table, seating him across from Archie.

I whispered to Greg, "What's going on?"

He held up a finger over his lips, but muttered, "You're about to hear it all right from his mouth."

Mom's eyes widened. We stood off to the side, riveted by what was about to come.

"Spill it, Larry," JJ demanded.

"You ratted me out?" Larry glared at Greg.

JJ got his attention. "Larry, tell me what happened on that mountain. The truth this time. And what does *this guy* have to do with it?"

Larry shook nervously under Archie's glare. He knew he had no choice though. "He was with two other guys on the mountain."

"How'd you meet them?"

"The first night we were here—after not being able to check into our rental—I went for a walk. I needed fresh air; I'd been traveling with the family all day—you know, with the parents and all." He paused, taking a deep breath. "After walking around the block, I came back into the cul-de-sac and saw him and another guy standing on the street. I recognized they could be the type of people who could help me find..." he paused, looking at Greg.

"To find what?"

"Something to ease my pain."

Greg smacked the kitchen countertop, causing us all to jump. "Jesus, Larry! Are you using again?"

"No!" he spat back at Greg. "But my back hurts. Especially after travel. Then learning that I'd have to sleep on the sofa that night! All I wanted was some pain relief."

JJ interjected, trying to minimize the family drama. "So, you approached the two men and you what? Asked them for *what type* of drugs?"

"I wanted some oxy."

"And? Did they hook you up?"

"No, but they said they could get me something even better. Only not until the next day."

"Archibald, is that correct?" JJ startled him by calling out his proper name. "Is that how it went down?"

He only shrugged.

"What happened then, Larry?"

"I went back to Libby's—slept uncomfortably all night." He turned to me. "No offense, Libby … it's just my back, and no matter where I sleep, it hurts."

JJ was getting impatient again. "Larry—spit it out. I want the entire story. Were these the same men who beat the hell out of you on the mountain?"

He nodded, cautiously glancing at Archie. "Yes. I met them at sunset on that crosscut trail, exactly where they told me. When I arrived, there was one ginormous man with them I hadn't met before. That startled me and I questioned who he was. Oh, they didn't like that. But also, in hindsight, I think they'd planned to rob me all along. They had no intention of giving me the drugs."

JJ motioned for him to tell more. From there, the whole beating, chasing up the mountain, and all the damage they'd done to Greg's brother was the story he'd told before. Turns out, he'd conveniently only left out the part that it was a drug deal gone bad. I felt for Greg; Larry's revelations clearly sickened him.

Archie wasn't nearly as defiant as when JJ initially seated

him at my table. After Larry's confession, JJ turned his strategy to playing the good cop, sympathizing with Archie, and trying to get more information on the Santos boys. Thankfully, it turned out that Archie was more concerned about his family life and ultimately being imprisoned. It wasn't long before the entire story spilled out in front of all of us.

We learned that the eldest Santos son, Carlos, had been friends with Archie dating back several years prior when they worked together at a delivery service. Carlos never cared for the man's wife, Robin, who was the nauseating, happy homemaker, in his eyes. When Archie showed signs of weakness during several of their men's happy hour outings after work, Carlos prompted Archie to engage in some illicit affairs. He'd made copies of keys to several properties his dad maintained. Over the years, this became a routine, to the point where Carlos ensured that Archie always had a place he could take his hook-ups. And best yet, Carlos was involved with one of the cleaning crew's women—everything was cleaned and kept secret, all the business under the table.

That grabbed my attention. "Surely Kaya knew about that? The crew would need to be paid."

"Carlos took care of it all. He has way more money than his father, Tiago—in fact, that house his dad has— paid for by Carlos. He's part of a Mexican drug cartel." Archie shivered sharing that bit. He looked JJ in the eyes. "I need protection. If they find out I talked, I'm as dead as that woman."

"Who killed Carol Linton?" I asked.

"I don't know!" His head hung low now. "We were going to have such a nice evening. She was so cute—still in her country outfit, boots and all, after line dancing class with a friend of hers. I'd prepared Chicken Piccata, my specialty. I was sure she'd stay the night with me."

"Where did it go wrong?"

"We'd had a glass of wine. Enjoyed the dinner; it was good, and she gave compliments. But she hadn't loosened up at all and she had *so many* questions for me." His mood shifted from reminiscing and took a dark turn. "I felt sure she'd leave me. This one was really pretty—smoking body, you know. I couldn't let her get away."

"What'd you do?"

"When she went to the bathroom, I slipped something into her wine to help her relax—just a little. I swear, my intention was only to provide a relaxer. Ultimately, I convinced her to stay by asking if she'd teach me about country dancing. We put on some music, we danced and drank. Until she fell to the floor."

"What did you do then?"

"I felt so bad." He sighed, and his eyes cast down at the table again. "I laid her out on the sofa to sleep for the night."

"That's it? How did she end up dead in the bathtub then?"

The long interrogation weighed on him. "I don't know," he said solemnly. "I keep questioning myself about that, but I swear she was alive the last time I saw her. She was breathing."

"Does that mean you left the house?" JJ paced around the table again.

Archie nodded. "You see, my wife called me all upset. One of my kids was ill, and she didn't know what to do. To back up a bit, I'd told her I had to work the night shift that night. Usually, I told her I was traveling." He cleared his throat before continuing. "I figured Carol was out cold, so I would run home and see about the family and I'd be back before she woke up. When I got back, though, she was gone."

"You checked the whole house?"

He shook his head. "I went into the living room and didn't find her on the couch. Her purse was gone off the kitchen counter where I'd seen it earlier, so I just assumed."

"Her car wasn't in the driveway?"

"I don't remember. I parked on the street, closest to the front door. You know how…"

JJ cut him off, giving him a dismissive hand gesture. "Yeah, yeah. But you didn't check the bedroom or anywhere else in the house?"

"No. I left, thinking she woke up and thought I'd deserted her. Okay, so I was afraid. I mean, jeez … I'd just drugged a woman!"

"You're telling me you've never done that before?"

He looked surprised. "Drugged a woman? No! But Carlos was always giving me these tips … you know, how to make dates *easier*."

"Oh, my God!" I exclaimed from the sidelines. "That's horrible!"

JJ shot a look in my direction and continued with his interrogation.

"So, what's your theory? Who killed Carol Linton if you had nothing to do with it?"

"Carlos's men."

"And how do you know that?"

"When we were on the mountain—after this clown." He pointed to the other end of the table. "Carlos directly said it—for us all to hear. It was horrifying, really. I thought I'd known the man. But he's not the same person I used to know. Ever since his involvement with the cartel … he's scary. I mean it—I need protection. I've already said way too much."

I had a hunch. "How is all this related to the burglary right here at my house?"

Larry flushed.

Archie gave a crooked smile and turned to Greg. "Well, *your brother*, in desperation, mind you, told us he had written information that could get us all in trouble. He tried threatening us with 'my brother's friends with the cops' … yeah, Carlos didn't like that."

"It was you who cut my lock, who was in my backyard before my dog scared you off, wasn't it? What exactly were you going to do that day?"

He shrugged.

"And exactly what was your plan for breaking in tonight?" I said, pointing to the broken window. It was already nearly two in the morning and I'd had enough when all he did was shrug off my question again. I wanted this slimy man out of my home. "JJ, can you get him out of here? I think there's enough for an arrest, don't you? We're all witnesses."

"Yep, we've got plenty to hold him on breaking and entering. And the list *will* continue. Archibald, you have the right to remain silent…" he stood the man up, finished reading him his rights, and walked him to the front door. JJ turned back. "Larry, don't go anywhere. We still need to talk."

Greg and Larry were in spirited conversation in the living room when Mom and I retreated to our rooms again.

It was mere hours before we were to be at Sage's house. I couldn't believe it was Thanksgiving Day. The rain had slowed, but was still a constant drumming on the roof. There was an occasional rumble of thunder, but all in the distance now. All I wanted to do was fall asleep. Within minutes of laying my head down, that's exactly what happened.

Until Shadow's barking woke me *again*.

CHAPTER TWENTY-FIVE

Shadow, Greg, and I sprinted into the darkness, our breaths coming in sharp puffs of steam in the cold, humid night air. The distant rumble of thunder filled the silence, but there was an urgency in our steps as we hurried down the street.

Shadow's ears perked up, her nose twitching, and she pulled ahead, leading us toward a copse of trees in the community park.

"Larry!" Greg shouted, but there was no response—only the sound of our feet splashing through the wet grass.

Suddenly, Shadow let out a low growl. Her hackles rose, and then we saw Larry stumbling out from behind some shrubbery, clutching his side. There was a wild, desperate look in his eyes.

"They're right behind me," Larry gasped. "We need to go now!"

Before any of us could react, headlights cut through the darkness in the opposite direction. A black SUV screeched to a halt, and two men stepped out, their silhouettes ominous. One of them cocked a gun, the sound echoing through the night.

Greg pulled Larry behind him. "You're not taking him!"

The leader of the group sneered, "That's not your decision to make."

I glanced at Shadow, who was poised and ready to protect. "We have to get out of here," I whispered to Greg, my heart hammering in my chest.

Greg scanned the area, eyes darting between the thugs and a narrow pathway from the community park out into the desert. "You know those trails better than anyone, right?" he whispered to me.

I nodded. "If we can get out there, I know exactly where to go. But what about Larry's foot?"

The leader stepped forward, pointing his gun at Larry. "No more games. Hand him over."

Just as Greg took a step back, preparing to grab Larry and make a run for it, Shadow lunged forward, barking ferociously. The sudden movement startled the men, and one of them fired a shot into the air.

"Go! Now!" Greg shouted, shoving Larry in my direction. I grabbed his arm, practically dragging him, as Greg stayed behind, swinging a branch he grabbed from the ground to keep the cartel members at bay.

We bolted through the narrow passageway, immediately hanging right, and Shadow darted ahead of us, dragging her leash behind but guiding the way. My heart raced, each step feeling like it might be the last, as the shouts of the cartel men faded into the background.

"We will not outrun them," Larry panted, clutching his side. "They'll find us."

"Not if we lose them first," I insisted, pushing him forward. "Just keep moving!"

Greg caught up to us, his breathing ragged but his eyes determined. "Over that hill!" he pointed out.

Without hesitation, we launched ourselves over a hill and plunged right into the cold water that filled the arroyo. Wading upstream as quickly as we could, Shadow paddled effortlessly beside me, her dark coat blending into the night.

We ducked behind a pile of washed-up debris, trying to muffle our breathing as a dark figure appeared high above. We heard them rustling to break through the thick desert brush along the bank. I held my breath, gripping Shadow's collar, then quietly shushing her. Brilliant light swept past us, illuminating the deep walls of the arroyo, but missing our exact hiding spot.

We heard cursing as they argued, their voices growing fainter as they moved farther away. Finally, silence settled over the desert once more, with only the occasional rumble of the distant thunder.

"We're not out of this yet," Greg murmured, wiping away the drips that fell from his hairline. "But they will not find you, Larry. Not if I have anything to say about it."

Larry nodded, still catching his breath. "I didn't think you'd come for me."

"That's what family does," Greg replied, determination etched in his face.

"How did you know he'd left?" I asked.

"Shadow's barking. I got up to see what got her wound up and heard scuffling outside in our front yard. Larry wasn't on the couch."

I nodded, remembering walking out into the living room and seeing Greg pulling on a jacket and his shoes. Quickly, I threw on some clothes and ran out the front door with him, not knowing where we were going.

For the moment, everything was silent except the sound of the water flowing and the occasional distant thunder.

I looked at Greg, then over at Larry. "We're not safe yet," I whispered. "But we're going to get you out of this."

Larry nodded, swallowing hard. "Thank you both," he breathed.

With Shadow leading the way again, we slipped out of the crevice and continued along the wash, keeping to the shadowed edges and out of the water, hoping to find safety.

Eventually, we reached the edge of my neighborhood again, with no concept of how much time had passed. Skirting through the darkness of the neighbors' yards, we saw the faint glow of what might have been a car's running lights in the distance. As we got closer, I noticed a vehicle parked along the road just outside my cul-de-sac.

"They're already here," Greg whispered, his jaw tightening. "We need to be smart about this. I'm sure they are waiting for us at the house."

"My mother is inside!" My eyes scanned the area again, with my mind racing uncontrollably. "We can't just walk up to the house. They'll be waiting. But what if they've already got my mom?" I pulled out my phone, wondering if it still worked. When I pushed the on-button, the screen illuminated. Remaining hopeful, I placed a call, dialing 911. The call wouldn't connect. I tried again but quickly gave up and hurriedly typed JJ a text message, briefly explaining.

Greg turned to me. "Texting, really?"

"JJ—for help."

"Libby, call 911!"

"I tried! Ok, I'll try again…" When the operator came on the line, I gave him my address, explaining we had intruders and asked for help right away, then hung up.

Unsure what would come next, I reached out for Shadow; she was tense and alert, every muscle in her body coiled and ready to spring.

"We've got to make sure Mom is okay."

"Is there a back entrance?" Larry asked.

Greg reminded him about the plywood covering over the back door.

"We can go through the basement!" I exclaimed.

"How did I not know about a basement?" Greg looked bewildered.

"Well, okay, I exaggerated. It's more of a crawl space, but I know we can get into the house through it."

Anxious about wasting more time, also worried about my mom, he stood. "Lead the way."

Crouching low, tiptoeing through the neighbor's bushes, we made it to the side of my home undetected. Carefully, we quieted our footfalls on the gravel, then through the gate, and I led them to the spot in the backyard. Kneeling down below the patio steps, I cautiously slid the latch to the side. The wooden door creaked, but I quickly got it opened and set it aside.

After hesitating for a moment to see if we had been detected, Greg signaled with his hand for us to crawl into the space. I shook my head, remembering the creepy crawlies from the water meter box. I offered for him to take the lead instead. Larry bowed out, unsure he could manage with his booted foot. Shadow and I followed Greg into the darkened tunnel.

As we reached the farthest end of the crawl space, we found the hatch-like door.

"Where does this put us in your house?" Greg asked.

"The laundry room, so, nearest the garage."

As he carefully lifted it, we heard voices.

"You're sure they'll come back here?" one man asked, his tone impatient.

"They've got nowhere else to go," another replied. "We just have to wait."

"But Carlos … c'mon, just let the oxy guy go. Archie's already arrested—he's goin' down for that broad's murder. Plus, he already told us this clown doesn't know a thing. He was at the wrong place at the wrong time, that's it."

"No, you idiot! He *said* he knew everything we did! Remember, on the trail that day … stupid punk. Besides, we can't get arrested for his assault. Then they'll have our DNA."

"I'm the idiot? If you'd only left the body alone and told your dad about letting Arch in his rental, we could have had him take the fall. None of this would be our problem now."

"Our DNA is all over that problem, bro."

"Well, what's done is done. These fools don't know about how you had your way with Archie's girl, though."

"I think they do! And now they can identify us."

"Well, the red head certainly could, you imbecile!"

I felt a chill creep down my spine, imagining what they did to Carol, and how afraid my mother must be inside with these horrible men. I exchanged a look with Greg, who raised a finger to his lips. He carefully lifted the panel soundlessly and set it aside. We paused, waiting for any reaction.

As the men continued their arguing, Greg slid himself up into the laundry room, seeing that the laundry room door was closed, but not latched. I peeked through the opening in the floor and my eyes flew open when I saw my mom cowering in the small space between the washer and a wall. Hefting myself up through the opening, Greg's eyes meet both of ours, warning us to stay quiet. I went over to her, reaching out for her hands, whispering ever so softly, "Shhh. We'll be okay. Help is on the way."

I peered down into the hole again, signaling to Shadow to wait. We carefully put our ears to the door, listening for our captors. Then I cracked the door open slightly. Through the small opening, I saw the two men in our living room, guns in hand, still arguing. I motioned for Greg to take a look.

"We can't fight them head-on," Greg whispered, his voice barely audible. "We need a distraction."

I got right up in his ear and whispered directly. "I say we just wait here until the police arrive. As long as we keep quiet, we're safest here."

He leaned over, whispering in my ear now. "Actually, since we found your mom—let's get her down into the crawlspace. Let's all get to safety."

Mom's eyes were wide, knowing we were devising a plan. I signaled for her to stand. She shook her head no, so

I went over and grabbed for her hand to help her up. She kept shaking her head, frozen with fear.

Greg tried whispering. "Julia, we've got to go!"

My heart clamored when I heard the man's voice.

"What was that? Did you hear that?" he said to his cohort.

My eyes implored my mom to get up. She cautiously stood, and Greg helped her down into the space with Shadow.

Footfalls on the tiled flooring were coming closer.

Greg scurried to get me down under floor and quickly lowered himself as well, quietly pulling the panel back in place seconds before the laundry room door opened.

I was sure they'd figure it out so I pressed the others to scoot all the way back through the crawl space. We emerged from underneath the back patio in time to hear sirens growing louder. The flashing lights bathed the neighborhood in an eerie glow, but for the first time in hours, I felt a flicker of hope. We'd made it through the night.

Larry dropped to the ground, his back against the house, tears of relief streaming down his face. "I thought it was all over. I knew they'd kill me."

"You're safe now," Greg assured him. "At least from the cartel."

CHAPTER TWENTY-SIX

Sage stood in her living room, smoothing the creases of her long, flowing sundress for what felt like the hundredth time. The Thanksgiving Day parade was already playing on the TV. She took a deep breath, trying to remind herself that today was about family and gratitude, not about the chaos her friends had been through.

The doorbell rang, and she plastered on a welcoming smile as she pulled it open. Dana stood there, balancing a tray of appetizers in one hand and holding her youngest son's hand in the other. "The others are following behind," Dana said breathlessly. "You know how it is, getting everyone out the door. And Joe's still not here—his flight got delayed."

Sage gave her a reassuring hug. "Come on in! Libby

isn't here yet either. Apparently, they had quite the drama last night."

"Oh no! What happened?"

"I'm sure we'll all learn about it later. For now, come in … grab coffee or a mimosa over there," Sage pointed out the drink station she'd set up. "Cody and Brad will be here soon to fix lefse for everyone."

"Lefse?"

"You'll see. It's delicious."

Dana's two kids ran inside and straight through the house to the open back door.

"I hope that's okay?" Dana followed them to the door and saw there was plenty of enclosed space for them to play. She quickly glanced at her phone, sighing deeply before forcing a smile.

"Oh, of course. They'll wear themselves out running around." Sage laughed, and turned to find Lexi, Joshua, and Bella walking through the front door.

"Welcome!" Sage guided them inside.

Next, Cody and Brad arrived, bursting through the doorway like a whirlwind of laughter and energy. "Happy Thanksgiving!" Brad boomed, thrusting a bouquet of flowers at Sage, while Cody balanced two bottles of wine and the casserole dish stacked with lefse. "We're here to eat, drink, and be merry!"

"More like eat, drink, and steal the show," Lexi muttered playfully as she came up behind Sage, earning a laugh from everyone.

Cody turned to Sage. "Better get the lefse going. Show me the way!" He glanced around the room. "Hey, where's Libby and Greg?"

"Don't worry, they're on their way."

Jordan and her kids arrived next, bringing their own rush of energy into the house. She hugged Sage tightly, handing her a bottle of wine, and quickly followed her children to the backyard where they found Dana's family.

The squeal of youthful voices abundantly filled Sage's home. She smiled at hearing Jordan's son, Chase, question the others.

"Hey, where's Shadow?"

Joey, Dana's son, stated matter-of-factly, "She caught the bad guys last night; she'll be here soon."

A rotund woman appeared at the front door screen, appearing apprehensive. Sage opened the door, "Welcome!"

Melissa looked a little fragile but managed a smile. "Thank you for having me. I'm Melissa Barnstead," her voice was soft, as she handed Sage a bottle of champagne. "I wasn't sure what to bring … is Libby here?"

"Melissa! Of course. Libby told me you'd be here. She's on her way." Sage ushered her inside. "I can't imagine what you've been through."

The older woman looked confused by Sage's meaning.

"Oh, I mean," Sage touched her arm in comfort, then turned to make sure no one overheard. She whispered, "You know, finding a dead woman in your rental property. That's horrifying!"

She nodded. "Of course. Yes, it was. Thankfully, we weren't the ones to find the poor woman. But, nevertheless, it's been quite the week." Her head hung in despair.

"Well, welcome to my home. We're going to have better energy here today." Sage pulled her in for a hug. "There's a drink station over there—mimosas, bloody marys, coffee, teas…whatever you want. Please make yourself at home."

Bill and Anne were the next to arrive, followed closely

by Larry, who hung back a little, hands shoved deep in his pockets. The tension crackled in the air the moment they stepped inside. "Hello, dear," Anne said, her voice warm, but her eyes distant as she scanned over the room.

Bill shook Sage's hand. "Thank you for having us." His eyes were also exploring, looking for Libby and Greg as they made their way inside. Noticing that Larry lagged behind, he quipped, "Try not to disappear before dinner this time, huh?"

Greg, Mom, JJ, Shadow, and I walked in just in time to feel the tension between the father and his son. I stepped forward quickly, trying to diffuse it. "Larry, it's great to see you. How's the foot doing this morning? Hopefully, you haven't injured it worse, I know last night was a lot."

He nodded, staring down at the medical boot on his foot. "I'm fine; I'm just glad it's all over." His eyes met JJ's, looking for affirmation on that point. JJ gave a slight nod.

Bill hugged Greg and me both, then shook hands with JJ. Shadow let out a whine. As soon as I released Shadow, she ran right toward the squeals heard in the backyard.

Officer Ortega made his entrance last, tapping on the doorframe as he entered. "Hey, I hope I'm not crashing the party," he said with a teasing grin on his face. "I came for the turkey…and to make sure no one gets arrested this year."

Larry's lips twitched, his eyes darted around nervously, clearly aware of his parents' watchful gaze.

"Ortega!" JJ exclaimed, taking his hand and enveloping him in a hug. "Glad you could make it, man."

JJ introduced him to everyone and we made our way to the drink station.

"Alright, everyone," I called out, clapping my hands

to gather their attention. "Welcome! Let's make this a Thanksgiving to remember!"

Greg squeezed my hand, whispering as he kissed the top of my head, "You've got this."

I smiled up at him, and for just one moment, I forgot about my aching body and everything that had occurred only hours prior.

The smell of butter and cinnamon filled the air. Soon, we snacked on lefse, with some of the group watching the parade on TV in the living room, and others lounging on the back patio. All the kids and Shadow remained playing outside; Cody brought them their own plate of the warm spicy flatbread. When Ryan, my sister's youngest, dropped his piece, Shadow swooped in and cleaned it right up.

I helped Sage get the turkey prepped and ready to go in the oven. We still had a couple hours before it'd go in, but she explained it would be good to let it rest at room temperature. In the meantime, we began heating the pre-made dishes and then added them to the warming trays Sage had set out along her gorgeous buffet table.

The crowd lingered around another buffet station out on the patio, where Sage had already set up appetizers—the pigs-in-a-blanket, deviled eggs, lefse, a vegetable tray, and an assortment of olives, nuts, and dried fruits.

I turned to Sage. "I'm so sorry and feel horrible we weren't here earlier to help you set up as we'd promised."

"Honey, you don't have to apologize. You had your hands full last night. Did you get any sleep at all?"

"Barely. Maybe two hours?"

"Oh, jeez, Libby. How are you functioning?"

"Adrenaline maybe." I chuckled, scanning the crowd. "Thank you, Sage. You saved Thanksgiving, and this is better than I could have ever hoped for. It's exactly as I imagined it should be."

Sage opened a cabinet nearest her. With a serene smile on her face, she showed me a bundle of dried herbs. "For protection and harmony," she explained. "The energy today feels a little heavy, but I think we can turn it around."

I had no idea what Sage meant, but I watched her light it and walk casually through the room. A light sage and lavender scented smoke followed her as she walked through the house. No one was the wiser. Or maybe they just accepted it as Sage being Sage.

As the morning wore on, cliques of friends gathered in small groupings around the property, snacking on appetizers, enjoying their beverages, and chatting while the main dishes finished cooking. The clinking of glasses, bursts of laughter, and the mouthwatering aroma of roasted turkey filled the air. Yet, despite the festive atmosphere, there was a clear tension that hovered around Larry and his parents.

Larry sat in a corner, picking at the deviled eggs on his plate, his shoulders hunched as if trying to make himself smaller. Anne couldn't seem to stop glancing his way, her lips pressed together tightly. Finally, she couldn't hold back any longer.

"Larry," she said, her voice edged with forced politeness, "could you please try not to eat all the appetizers before dinner? You know you have to leave some for the others."

Larry's jaw clenched, and he put down the egg he had just picked up. "I'm not eating them all, Mother," he muttered, clearly irritated at being treated like a child. "I've only had a few."

Bill jumped in, his tone sharper. "You know it wouldn't

kill you to be more considerate. We're not asking much, Larry."

"Okay, Dad, got it," Larry shot back, his voice rising. "I'll just sit here and not touch anything, or say anything, alright? Would *that* make you happy?"

The room fell silent. All eyes flickered toward Larry and his parents; the tension was so thick it was nearly suffocating. I exchanged a worried glance with Greg, who looked ready to intervene, but Cody was faster.

"Whoa, whoa, whoa!" Cody called out, clapping his hands together playfully. "Hold up. Is this the kind of Thanksgiving we're having? Because I thought this was the 'stuff-your-face-and-laugh-till-you-cry' kind of day, not the 'everyone-get-all-serious' kind."

Brad, catching on quickly, grabbed one of the deviled eggs off Larry's plate and stuffed it into his mouth. "Mmm," he said, exaggerating his chewing. "Larry, I gotta say, you've got excellent taste in appetizers. You should be the official taste-tester for this family."

Cody nodded enthusiastically. "Yes! In fact, I hereby declare Larry the 'Deviled Egg King' of Thanksgiving!" He grabbed a cloth napkin, twisted it into a makeshift crown, and placed it on Larry's head. "All hail King Larry!"

The room erupted in laughter, and even Larry couldn't help but crack a reluctant smile. "You guys are ridiculous," he said, but at least there was warmth in his eyes now.

Brad wasn't done. "Ridiculously amazing, you mean," he quipped. "But really, if you don't taste everything first, how will we know it's good enough to eat?"

Sage chimed in. "Larry, it's obviously your calling. The universe clearly brought you here today for this important role."

Even Anne, who had been fuming just moments before, let out a little chuckle, her shoulders relaxing. Bill sighed, shaking his head, and there may have been a slight smile emerging.

"Alright, alright," Larry said, adjusting his napkin crown. "I'll accept the job. But I expect full control over the egg supply from now on."

"Done!" Cody agreed, lifting his wineglass in a toast. "To King Larry, the Deviled Egg Connoisseur!"

Everyone joined in, and the tension melted away, replaced by genuine laughter and a renewed sense of togetherness. As the conversation resumed and everyone settled back into the comfortable chatter, Cody shot a quick wink at Larry, who mouthed a silent, "Thank you."

The moment passed, and the warmth of the gathering took over again, stronger than the lingering shadows of past hurts.

CHAPTER TWENTY-SEVEN

Dana stood by the kitchen window, gazing out at the cloudy sky with her phone in hand. She'd been checking it every few minutes, hoping for some word from her husband, but so far, nothing. She took a deep breath, trying to push down the lump in her throat.

Jordan noticed her standing there alone and walked over, offering a sympathetic smile. "Hey," she said softly. "You doing okay? Looks like our kids have made fast friends this week."

Dana forced a smile, but her eyes were glassy. "I'm fine. Just wish Joe could be here, you know? It's hard, him always traveling. The kids miss him, and… well, so do I."

Jordan nodded, leaning against the counter. "I can't imagine how tough that must be. But you're incredibly strong, Dana. I can tell that, even in the short time I've known you. It takes a lot to keep everything together when he's away. I know, as a single mom."

Dana let out a shaky laugh. "Sometimes I wonder if I am? Strong, that is. I just get tired of doing it all on my own. As you well know."

Jordan reached out, squeezing Dana's hand. "It's okay to feel that way. You don't have to be superwoman all the time. And hey, we're all here for you today. You're not alone."

Dana blinked back tears, giving Jordan a grateful smile. "Thank you. That means a lot."

"Anytime," Jordan replied, pulling her in for a quick hug. "Besides, I have a feeling Joe's going to surprise you today. Call it sisterly intuition."

Dana laughed, the tension easing. "I hope you're right."

I walked in. "Hope she's right about what?" I asked.

"Joe making it in time for turkey."

I checked my watch, smiling knowingly. "I'm sure he will."

JJ interrupted, asking to speak to me in private. I followed him out the front door. Greg and Larry were already out there. We all took seats on the patio.

"I know today is about family and not all the nasty business we've been dealing with this week. So, I'll keep it brief… I thought you'd be pleased to hear that we have successfully placed Archie, Carlos, and the other Santos son, Miguel, in jail. You have nothing to worry about. Tomorrow, they will arraign them and the prosecutor informed me they will recommend no bail because of the flight risk.

Larry let out a tremendous sigh. "That's such a relief."

Greg patted his back. "And as you've already agreed to, you'll go home and seek the care of a doctor to overcome this back pain. No more drugs."

"Promise, brother." His eyes held Greg's with appreciation.

"Will the confession we overheard hold up in court?" I asked JJ. "Carlos admitted to killing that woman."

"I sure hope so. You all will have to testify. That's down the road, but at least the prosecution has your statements. It will go a long way to securing their sentences."

"I feel bad for Archie," Greg stated.

"Why? I don't!" I retorted. "The guy was cheating on his wife and got an innocent woman murdered!"

Greg nodded. "Yes, I know. I only meant that I believe he never *meant* for the woman to be killed."

JJ added. "He should have never given her Rohypnol. That stuff is dangerous. Plus, you have to question why a man conveniently has a drug like that on hand. He's not an innocent person."

"Oh, I didn't know that part." Greg took my hand. "We'll have to check in with his wife. Poor thing, left with all those kids to take care of."

I nodded, still stunned by the turn of events. "Hey, there was something about strangulation—you know, in the autopsy report. So, it wasn't really an overdose, and we heard Carlos admitting to killing her. Did he strangle her with his hands? I suppose he's big and strong enough to."

JJ shook his head. "She had on a country-western outfit. From photos we found on her phone from earlier that evening, it looks like she'd been out dancing. In fact, I think Archie said something about that, right? Well, anyway, she had a red bandanna around her neck. I suspect he used that—maybe even grabbed it if she had tried to run away from him?"

My pulse quickened. I wasn't sure if I should divulge, but then realized it could be crucial to the investigation. I turned to Larry.

"Remember that bandanna Shadow found in your bag when you came home from the hospital?"

He nodded. "Yeah, I do not know where that came from."

"I know! After those thugs assaulted you and you got rescued from the mountain, think about it. Later, the hospital staff gathered your personal effects and put them in a bag before releasing you. That's how it got to the house."

Greg caught on to my train of thought and remembered something. "Larry, you had that in your hand when we found you on the mountain. You wiped your forehead with it. Where did you find it?"

His gaze scanned the horizon, looking out over the same mountain range where he'd spent a couple nights wounded and lost. He slowly shook his head. "My memory still isn't great. I suppose I found it?"

"Or one of your assailants dropped it." And then an even worse thought occurred. "What if they *planted it* on you?"

JJ interrupted. "Where is it now?"

We all turned and stared blankly at him.

I thought about it for a second. "It's got to be at the house."

"And is that what they were looking for when they broke into your house?"

"Were they the ones who broke into my house?"

"We think it was Archie, but just go along with me on this."

I thought back to the timing of events. "No. Someone broke into my house while Larry was missing." I turned to Greg. "And the bandana was definitely at the scene when you found Larry—you just said."

Greg remembered something. "Libs, didn't Carlos—or maybe it was Archie—mention something last night about evidence Larry had back at the house?"

"Yes! There was something like that."

Larry piped up. "I was bluffing. I had nothing, but I hoped they would take me back to town. My reasoning was that going back to the city would increase my chances of getting help. I'm sorry they trashed your house, Libby."

JJ held up a finger. "Okay, we're not going to completely solve this right here. But, when we leave here today, I need to get that bandanna from you. We'll get forensics on it."

"Larry's DNA is all over it," Greg said.

JJ shrugged. "And we'll report that. However, if the woman's and Carlos' DNA is found on it, that will place everyone at the crime scene. Which will make it a much stronger case."

My spirits lifted. I knew right where I'd set that piece of cloth and thankfully, I hadn't washed it. Then I remembered something.

"What about the white van? Did you ever connect that to either of the crimes?"

JJ nodded. "It's your neighbor's—Archie's."

My jaw dropped. "How had I not known that?" I thought about it for a second. "Wait a minute, I remember seeing a large white vehicle backing into their garage a couple of days ago. *That* was the van?"

My friend nodded again. "Yep. That's why it was found on camera in your cul-de-sac. Honestly, it surprised me it wasn't captured in more footage … or that the other neighbors didn't identify it as Archie's. When I asked, I learned it was his work van. He only rarely drove it home."

"Oh!" I lowered my voice and leaned in toward JJ. "Did you ever get that text I sent with Fred Barnstead pictured with Carol Linton on Instagram?"

"I did, and we've cleared Fred from all wrongdoing. I mean, I don't know what's going on between him and his wife, but he told me that picture was one they took in celebration of a property he'd sold to Carol. He was distraught that she was the woman who turned up dead."

"Whoa, that's a random entanglement." I considered whether I believed that story. "And back to Carlos and his goons. Why leave the woman's body in the house?"

"We haven't got that out of them yet. My theory is that the Lawsons showed up before they could get her out. I have to check on the timing of all that, but something prevented them from fixing their problem. Or, they set Archie up to take that fall?"

Greg, Larry, and I sat, considering all we'd learned. I couldn't ignore how easily Larry could have been set up in the whole debacle as well.

Our attention turned as a car drove into the driveway.

CHAPTER TWENTY-EIGHT

Dana was in the living room, half-heartedly listening to Cody tell a story about one of his latest adventures, when her phone buzzed. Her heart leaped, but it was just another promotional email. She sighed, rubbing her temples.

Suddenly, the front door swung open, and a gust of air blew through the house. "Hey, did someone call for an airline pilot?" a familiar voice called out.

Dana froze, her eyes wide. She whipped around to see Joe standing in the doorway, still in his uniform, his suitcase by his side, and a weary but beaming smile on his face. For a moment, she couldn't move, couldn't speak, as if she didn't believe he was really there.

"Joe?" she whispered, her voice catching. "I thought I

was going to pick you up?"

"Surprise!" he said, stepping forward. "I wouldn't miss Thanksgiving with my family."

Dana flew across the room and wrapped her arms around him, tears streaming down her cheeks. "You're here! I can't believe you're here!"

Joe hugged her tightly, lifting her off the ground for a moment. "I'm sorry I'm late, but I'm here now."

Dana looked up at him, her eyes shining with tears. "This is the best surprise ever," she said, brushing her hand against his cheek.

The room erupted into cheers and applause, and the kids came running in from the backyard. "Dad!" Joey and Lila launched themselves into their father's arms. Joe smiled brightly, kissing their foreheads.

Dana started the introductions around the room and everything felt complete now.

As we enjoyed the bountiful turkey dinner, I listened as conversations swirled around the tables. Jordan and Dana bonded over parenthood as Joe and Greg got caught up with each other's lives. Melissa and Officer Ortega, or Jose, as he asked us to address him, found commonality with her newfound love of Mexico. I overheard him saying his family came from the state of Jalisco originally. Thankfully, Anne and Bill chilled out and seemed to enjoy their conversation with my mother. Greg had mediated a private conversation earlier with all of them outside, not long after Cody's intervention. Since then, everyone appeared much more relaxed.

I couldn't really blame anyone for the earlier tension.

This week had been *a lot*. Ever since the Lawsons' arrival, nothing had gone as planned. It wasn't as if we could keep up the false pretenses for long. Eventually, true raw emotion was bound to overflow. Spontaneously, I gently clinked my wine glass with my fork. When everyone on the patio quieted, I stood up.

"Friends. Family. Let's give Sage our warmest gratitude for saving this gathering that was nearly canceled." Everyone clapped, directing their thank-yous to Sage. She blushed, nodding her head. "The whole meaning of Thanksgiving is to gather with family—both our birth families and our chosen ones." I directly gazed at my dear friends, Lexi and her husband, JJ, sitting at my table. For them, my heart overflowed with love. And then my eyes scanned around to all those seated at other tables. Friends for many years to those I'd only made recently, I was so grateful for each one of them. "I'm so blessed to have you all here, to spend one day out of the busy year gathering together simply means the world to me. I want each of you to know how much I love you."

Awwws were voiced from around the patio.

"To our *family*!" I lifted my glass and we all toasted. "That's all—keep eating before it all gets cold!" I laughed and took my seat, leaning over to give Greg a kiss.

He froze for a second.

"What is it?" I asked.

He patted his pants pockets, then his shirt pocket.

My mom's hands covered her mouth and her eyes flew open.

Confused, I asked again. "What?"

He gave a slight nod, saying, "No, no. Nothing." Then his mouth found mine and he gave me a lingering kiss.

I heard a frustrated sigh from my mother as she went back to eating. There was something unspoken between my mother and Greg, I was sure of it. Instead of prying, I was only happy that the two got along famously. That was all I could ask for.

*　*　*

The next morning, the sun had barely risen, casting a soft, golden glow through the living room windows. I stood by the front door with Greg, as we waited for Larry and the family to load into the vehicles.

Anne was the first to step out, her expression warm but a little weary. "Thank you again for everything, Libby," she said, pulling me into a tight hug. "The food was wonderful, and … it was good for all of us to be together."

I smiled, hugging her back. "I'm so glad you came, but wish it were under better circumstances and that we'd had more one-on-one time. But we will next time."

Bill appeared next, carrying a bag of goodies we'd loaded them up with for the road trip. He gave Greg a firm handshake, his tone gruff but genuine. "Good to see you again, son. Take care of yourself … and don't screw it up with this one." He nodded toward me with a broad smile. "She's a keeper, son." They hugged, and then Greg turned to Larry.

He stepped forward and clapped a hand on his brother's shoulder. "Hey, don't be a stranger, alright? We'll catch up soon. Just … well, take care of yourself."

Larry swallowed hard and gave a quick nod. "I will." He hesitated, then added, "I'm … I'm gonna try harder this time. I don't want to mess up again."

Anne, overhearing, stepped closer, her voice soft but firm. "We believe in you, Larry. Just take it one day at a time. We'll be there for you through your recovery."

Dana, Joe, and their kids all gave us hugs, promising to have us to their home someday soon. For a moment they stood there; the unspoken weight of the family's struggle hung in the cool morning air. Then, breaking the silence, Mom came bounding out of the house with a leftover pie in hand, calling out, "Hey, before you leave, you have to take some of this! It's a crime to waste dessert!"

The tension lifted as everyone laughed, Julia thrusting the pie into Bill's hands. "Trust me, you'll regret it if you don't take this."

With a few more hugs and handshakes, the family climbed into their vehicles. The engines roared to life, and the kids rolled down the windows, giving everyone a final wave as the caravan rolled down the street.

As they pulled away, Greg and I watched in silence until they disappeared around the corner.

"He's going to be okay," I said, squeezing Greg's hand.

"I hope so," Greg's voice was wistful and a little strained. "He's trying. That's all we can ask for right now."

"I'm sorry they left early. But I certainly understand." I said as we walked back into the humid staleness of our home. "I hope we can get someone out to replace that sliding glass door soon."

My mom's head hung in despair. "There's so much to do here and at my home, too. I wish we could wave a magic wand."

"Me too, Mom. Me too."

"I appreciate you having me here though," she smiled. "So, where do we start?"

I looked around the room in despair. Then shook it off and smiled. "First, I'll call my insurance company. Then we'll head over to your house and begin clearing out your belongings for the storage unit."

Greg nodded. "JJ offered to help this weekend as well." He pulled out his phone and called our friend to set up a time.

* * *

Lexi's eyes were wide as they took in the full extent of the mess. My mother's house was a disaster.

"Have they found those guys who defrauded you?" she asked Julia, setting down her purse, before pulling her into a hug.

Mom shook her head. "They have a few leads, but nothing concrete yet."

JJ spoke up. "I'll follow up at the station. I'd bet anything they've done this before—we'll get them."

My heart bled for my mother, losing so much money.

After half an hour of being in my mother's home, with masks and gloves on, we'd finally settled into a routine of boxing up personal effects. Each room had several large boxes labeled Clean-Storage and For Restoration Cleaners. Greg and JJ helped my mother in the kitchen. I tackled the primary bedroom suite and Lexi was going through the living room shelves.

Once I got into my mom's closet, I knelt down and scooted several items aside, making it easier for me to reach the farthest recesses. As I reached for a couple of chairs stored in the corner, something caught my eye. A small, locked chest, half-hidden under an old blanket. Brushing away the dust, my fingers traced the intricate carvings on the lid. *Where had* this *come from?*

I remembered from our ski vacation last winter, and the friendship I'd made with the nice baker, Samantha Sweet. She had a carved box. It was much nicer than this one. Even so, it reminded me of her. Curiosity piqued, and I tugged at the little lock. The lock was old and rusted, as though no one had opened it in years. With a quick glance behind me, I hesitated. I heard the footfalls and then saw my mom's disheveled appearance in the bedroom doorway.

"Hey mom!" I called out. "Have you seen this before?"

She came over and knelt down beside me. Suddenly, the atmosphere felt charged with an unsettling tension. "Where'd you find this?" she asked.

I pointed into the corner.

She pulled a hairpin from her pocket, the one she always used when her hair was misbehaving, and carefully began to pick the lock. My heart pounded a little faster with each click.

Just as the lock gave way with a soft snap, she pulled it from the clasp and lifted the lid slowly, revealing faded old letters and some photographs. Her breath caught as she recognized the handwriting on the envelope.

"Mom, what is it?" I whispered, my voice trembling slightly as she held up the bundle of letters.

For a moment, an expression of shock—perhaps even fear—crossed her face before she quickly composed herself. "I don't understand what this is doing here?"

With concern etched across my face, I asked, "What is this? It has to be yours if it's in your closet, right?"

She took a deep breath, her eyes narrowing slightly as she shook her head. "It's something that should have stayed buried, Libby. This … *this* is something I hoped our family would never have to deal with again."

The tension in the room thickened as the bundle trembled slightly in my mother's hand, the weight of an old, long-buried family secret threatening to unravel.

Julia Madsen hesitated, her fingers tightening around the envelope. After a moment, she let out a shaky sigh and handed it over to me. "I think it's time you knew the truth."

My heart raced as I carefully unfolded the aged paper. The handwriting was familiar, but shaky, as though written by someone in distress. As I read, my eyes widened in disbelief.

Dear Julia, if you're reading this, it means they found me. Please see that the contents of this box get distributed between Libby and Jordan when you deem the time is appropriate. I wish it could have been different, and I never got caught up in all this. I'm truly sorry. Leon.

"*Dad* left this note?" I whispered in disbelief.

Tears streamed from my mother's face as she nodded. "You were never meant to see this. But now that you have, can we keep it between the two of us?"

"What exactly did Dad mean by '*it means they found me*'? Who?"

Mom sighed deeply, her shoulders sagging as if the weight of the truth was too much to bear. I stared at her as she wiped tears away and spoke in a broken, weary voice.

"Your father … well, although the official cause of death was a heart attack, I don't believe it occurred naturally."

My throat felt like sandpaper and my legs were too weak to stand, despite my desperate need to get out of the closet. I rolled over onto all fours and used the doorframe to anchor myself as I stood. I sank into a nearby chair, holding my head in my hands. The reality of my father's death felt like a punch to my gut. "I don't understand. What exactly happened?"

Her eyes full of regret, Julia reached out for me.

"Libby, you were only a child. For a while, I also believed our whole family was in danger."

"*Danger?*"

"You know your father was an insurance adjuster. Unfortunately, he came across a situation. One that put his life in grave danger."

"Did someone threaten Dad's life?"

Julia nodded, and another tear escaped. "I thought that if you knew … it would change the way you saw him. Or maybe the way you remembered him. You idolized him, sweetie. Oh, he loved you so much."

I shook my head, tears streaming down my face. Completely betrayed, but also somewhat understanding of my mother's reasoning, the room filled with conflicting emotions—grief, anger, and a strange sense of empathy for my mother's impossible position.

She reached out for my hand, gripping it tightly.

"I'm sorry, Libby. I thought I was doing the right thing, but after so many years, I believed the story I told myself. It wasn't *untrue*. I only … well, it felt safer keeping it a buried secret."

"What exactly happened?" I was curious.

"To this day, I don't know all the details. Your father protected us by not giving me the particulars. I do know that something he learned from an insurance investigation got him in trouble with some unsavory people."

"Did they catch them?"

She slowly shook her head. "The coroner ruled his death a heart attack. There really wasn't anything for them to look into. Don't get me wrong. I went to the police, but all I had was the letter—no proof of any wrongdoing."

"No work notes?"

"I assumed the police spoke to your father's bosses and they'd turn over whatever was necessary. It wasn't enough to open a case, though. I guess."

"You asked that we keep this between us. Jordan doesn't know?"

She shook her head. "Neither of you girls."

"I wish you'd told me sooner, Mom. I feel lied to. But I … I understand. I just need some time. And we must tell Jordan. I'm not keeping this from her."

Julia's head fell forward. She squeezed my hand. Sitting in silence, holding hands, we grieved the loss of a man we both dearly loved. The truth was out, and now I had to figure out how I'd deal with it.

"What did he mean by, '*the contents of the box being divided*'? What was in it?" I asked.

"He'd set up trust accounts for both you and Jordan. You'll each receive access when you turn forty. It was important to us you forged your own way in life, but he also wanted to do a little something for his girls."

More tears flowed down my cheeks. "We need to call Jordan."

She agreed. "Let's not do this with the others here in the house. She's planning to come over tomorrow and help, anyway. We'll tell her then. Deal?"

I nodded, reading the note again before folding it and placing it back into the box. The thought was unbearable that my father's death may have been something more sinister. It felt like this had ripped old wounds wide open again. My head was still spinning with emotions I wasn't sure how to deal with. There was an anger at being deceived. I was also sad he must have been going through a particularly difficult time. Part of me denied this new revelation as truth.

My mom reached over for another hug. "I'm going to get back to the guys in the kitchen before they come looking for us. Will you be okay?"

I simply nodded and got back to my job.

It was several days later when I told Greg everything. He'd questioned several times why I was so quiet, but I couldn't open up until I'd processed my emotions. Jordan didn't believe any of it. She took being lied to far more personally, and even though I completely understood why, I prayed we could heal as a family.

We both felt a deep sense of sorrow for the time we'd lost, unable to fully come to terms with our father's death. It felt impossible to confront the complexities of losing our father too soon. That it could have come at the hands of criminals added another layer of grief. And my poor mother. She had all the same emotions, grieving while she carried on raising her daughters *and* trying to get the authorities to do something about it. I knew how impossibly difficult that had to have been for her.

* * *

Weeks later, Greg pulled me into his arms. "You're still struggling, aren't you?"

Whipping up some breakfast for us, I simply nodded. The tears had dried up days ago, but the sting in my heart was still there. I dished up our omelets, and we carried them outside to the patio table. Shadow followed at our heels.

The cool, but sunny morning was a welcome relief from the recent brutal summer. I pulled the sliding glass door closed, and we sat to soak in the sunshine.

While taking a bite of the cheesy egg dish, he mentioned how he missed having my mom around.

I nodded in agreement. "She didn't have to move over to Margie's house, but I understand."

"She was missing the old neighborhood before you ever found that note, hon. I mean, it's going to be several more weeks until her house is ready to move back into."

"I know."

"Okay. Different subject." His thousand-watt smile reflected the direct sunlight. "Let's do some desert-climate hiking!"

My eyes perked up.

"It's been a while. And after this crazy Thanksgiving we've experienced, I think we should get away for a few days—back into nature. Just the two of us."

"I agree. Where?"

"The Four Peaks Wilderness has always intrigued me and the temperatures work for winter hiking. Maybe we make a Christmas of it and completely abandon the idea of the typical family holidays."

My mind had been dreading the thought of another family gathering anytime soon. Christmas was less than a week away; way too close for comfort.

I turned to him eagerly, "Let's do it!"

He leaned over and planted a kiss before taking another swig from his coffee mug. "This will be one to remember." He sat back with a huge grin on his face.

* * *

Thank you for taking the time to read *Shadows Over Thanksgiving*. If you enjoyed it please tell your friends, and I would be so grateful if you would consider posting a review. Word of mouth is an author's best friend, and very much appreciated.
Thank you,
Jennifer Morgan

* * *

What's next for Libby and Shadow?

Libby always believed her father died of a tragic heart attack at a young age—until a hidden box she found reveals buried secrets. With her loyal Labrador, Shadow, and a close-knit circle of friends, Libby dives into a high-stakes investigation that stretches from corrupt boardrooms to desolate mountain trails. As mysterious forces close in, a long-lost truth emerges, and Libby finds herself facing more danger than she could have imagined.

When a mountain hike reveals a hidden amethyst mine—and a haunting mystery—Greg's plans for a proposal are temporarily put on hold. Determined to find that perfect moment, he stays resolute and keeps his eye on the prize.

In this adventure packed with rugged hikes, haunted mines, and a chilling conspiracy, Libby must risk everything to expose a truth that refuses to stay buried. Will she uncover the secrets that claimed her father's life—or will those who guard them silence her forever? Does Greg get the chance to propose?

Don't miss Book 10 in this "impressively original and deftly crafted"* series!

**Midwest Book Review*

Get another free book from Jennifer—click here to find out how!

Books in the Libby Madsen Cozy Mysteries series:
Shadows in the Forest
Spa Shadows
Shadowed Treasures
Shadow Retreats
Spooky Shadows
Shadow's Christmas Wish
Festive Shadows
Shadows in Alaska
Shadows Over Thanksgiving
The Christmas Fairy – a holiday novella

Let's connect!

Website: www.jenniferjmorgan.com
Email: jennifer@jenniferjmorgan.com
Facebook: .facebook.com/profile.
php?id=100076154359528
Twitter: twitter.com/JenniferJMorga3
BookBub: bookbub.com/profile/433830544
Goodreads: goodreads.com/user/show/148099219-
jennifer-morgan

* 9 7 8 1 6 4 9 1 4 1 9 9 6 *